Salty Beginnings

D.L. Barnes

Salty Beginnings

Second Edition

Books of the
Coastal Saga Series

Salty Beginnings

Burning Bush Bakery

Captain Bodacious

www.oceantimepublishing.com

Chapter 1

THERE WAS A CONSTANT breeze on Charley Howard's face as he jogged to the marina and back to his comfortable home that sat on a slight bluff off the fringes of where the tide eased in from the Atlantic. The sounds of peaceful birds chirping and water lapping against the cove's banks reflected a contrasting sensual experience to the clamor along the older streets of Savannah. To Charley, who had grown up in the area all of his life, it was like having a pot of spaghetti sauce on the stove. When things underneath got too hot, the only thing left was to spit out at whoever was close enough to take a hit or spill out over the kitchen stove, leaving someone a mess to clean. Therefore, Charley spent most of his days between pots trying to keep the spices of life working together. Most of the time, it worked, and everyone was pleased with the results. But, sometimes, his life was busy cleaning the stains that were part of the lives he encountered.

"Hey, Charley!" As he returned to his drive, his neighbor called from next door.

Charley waved and put his hands on his hips as he slowed down his pace to lower his respiration and his heart rate. He continued to have his daily ritual of exercises even in his middle years. He tried not to recall thoughts from his college days now. His neighbor, Bob, felt the same way.

"Thinking about going to church today?" Bob asked with a mischievous smile on his face.

Charley looked back at Bob and shook his head while getting himself back to normal breathing. "I suspect I will be there since I have the sermon."

"Yes, that is true, but I was hoping I could talk you into fishing with me and some buddies today. Let us help you get out and mix with people a bit."

Charley laughed. "When did I show signs of difficulties with social skills?"

"I'm just saying that all that work I see you do around town with no fishing out there in the rolling sea might be good for you. It would make me a little more obstinate in my job."

"I'm not sure what obstinate means in the dictionary, but I think I'm better off with a bit of it to keep me on the right track." Charley wiped the sweat off his brow.

Bob wasn't willing to cut his friend any slack, but

he also knew that Charley was a man who lived at the soul level. That's what made him different from most men. Perhaps everyone strives for that one factor, but few understand the source. "Charles Howard, my life's mission is to corrupt you, and I'm not succeeding today. But I must try harder to win my wings, you know."

"If it is a pair of wings you'll receive for helping me find trouble, you'll have a set of them soon enough."

"I like to know now and then that you're just like me."

"I'll take a rain check on fishing. Then, if you go out on another day of the week, call and let me know. By the way, you probably are a much better man than me most days, so don't get green-eyed on me. It just wouldn't be right. That's all I'm saying."

"Okay, I heard that!" Bob looked over at Charley before closing the trunk door of his vehicle. "You know, something has always had me stumped about you. Why did you become a minister? There would be double trouble around here if you were not so saintly all the time! A good-looking guy like yourself and a brainy guy like me behind the operations could have been the ticket to being the next tycoons!"

Charley laughed. "Bob, all my friends in my past made me the man I am today. I'm sure living next to you all these years has heavily influenced me to make tough choices. I'm thinking of one right now. Do I try out that new reel and rod that I received as a gift for my birthday, or do I go perform baby dedications by sprinkling water on innocent infants and making them cry? As a bachelor, that's a tough stretch. As a man who has made peace with God's plan, I am happy to do what I do."

"There you go. That's why we are different, my friend. Well, I've slowed you down enough this morning. I'll talk to you later."

Charley waved back, picked up the paper, and went into the house. He transformed into the man people had gotten used to seeing on Sunday mornings for the last 20 years.

It was a clear, crisp December morning, and Charley quickly put on his robes and stood on the church steps as he greeted guests at the door. He was now in his official attire, performing his duty as a seasoned warrior. The air swirled around the skirting of the pastor's robe as the breeze kicked up around the stoop of the church steps. Members and guests filtered by him while he pleasantly welcomed the attendees for the service. Some used the church title of pastor. Others identified him with Dr. Howard's additional formality because of his education level. Those who knew him outside of the church often called him Charley. Reverend Howard felt the most intriguing individuals were those who nodded as they whisked right on by finding a spot in the sanctuary. Those who came to the church on this square each Sunday were mixed. A few came with their families, and others came alone. They all had reasons for coming. Some in the congregation wore jeans to Sunday morning services, but suits and ties were no exception. The church assembly starkly contrasted with established neighborhoods with historical homes and moss-covered trees characteristic of the romantic Savannah and its traditions. The church on the corner was a safe place for those who looked for God but felt rejected by an established church. Charley envisioned that a church should be a place that fostered acceptance for those sincerely seeking to understand God's truths. Seeking meaning in one's life was an ongoing daily activity for the pastor. Years passed since Charley remained committed to walking down his chosen path. His original choice for his life had been a different road, but through a chain of events, he decided on a path, not knowing where it would lead. Of late, he struggled with those feelings within himself. Some people hike on a long path for months while others train for marathons reaching beyond the aches and strains towards that something. Charley understood the deep pangs of hunger for understanding. He, too, was a seeker of truth, and he befriended those who traveled the road with him.

Something unexpectedly extraordinary would touch Charley's stiffening heart on a particular Sunday in February. The first bolt of electricity came as the Reverend stood at the church entrance, greeting the guests. A couple quickly moved by him and touched the hand and the hem of his sleeve. He did not recognize them, but he felt a connection with what he rarely felt anymore. The man and woman went inside before he could process the experience. The next one in line shook the pastor's welcoming hand, and the moment was gone. The deacon signaled to Reverend Howard that it was time to escape to his office and make one last prayer before the morning service. It was his ritual, and Reverend Howard rarely deviated from duty or routine. He fell victim to supporting his broken family and denying his life's yearnings in his youth. His parents planted powerful feelings of guilt in Charley, as he was called by his parents when they were silently disappointed in his choices. He found challenging the family's traditions and behaviors futile if he wanted to avoid exile from his parents' love. He could not think badly of them, though, as Calvin and Gladys Howard were always perfect, or so he thought for many years. They were responsible parents who did all they could to bring up their son properly, with good intentions. However, breaking the family's rigid rules of conduct was unacceptable. Charley had kept the rules, mostly; however, smoldering ash was left in the heart of Reverend Howard as a young man while he was learning the ropes of life. He never spoke of it or acknowledged the wound that still festered. His memory hid one of those practiced but never said rules. Those who were not acceptable to the family's expectations were piled into a lump of evil sinners and losers, depending on how one would define the rejected group. Charley later challenged the rule of what was acceptable and valued as a family member as he made his way through life. Some minor decisions had unexpected consequences that snowballed and had a lasting effect on changing his life's direction. In Charley's mind, he had made peace with the conflict between the strict rules he grew up with and the message he wanted to share with others based on his faith. Lately, he had been facing another battle of sorts. He was growing empty from all the needs of others. The church staff asked more of him, and the number of parishioners' requests grew steadily. The community cried out about their needs all around him, and he wanted to ease their condition. With mounting demands, it became a burden to feel at all.

Reverend Howard briefly looked around the pews, smiling at the faces that field God's house. He had selected a sermon for dedicating babies to the church, a warm message with antidotes of parents' acts of selfless love. Perhaps it was not his best service, but it was based on all he had observed. At the end of the service, Reverend Howard walked to the back of the church, ready for handshaking and well wishes. There it was again. A flash of awareness, a spark of something, and the moment was gone. It happened once during the service as he glanced over at the congregation today. Charley stood at the back of the church, seeking to associate the spark with something or someone. It wasn't his imagination. Something had touched him and awakened him from his routine. Something had awakened the real Reverend Howard.

Michael and CeCe had walked from the church over a few blocks to a popular eating establishment in Savannah's historic district. The line was long to get a table. They could soak in the sunshine if they opted to watch from a sidewalk table.

Their story of why they were in Savannah began when Michael had moved back to Pennsylvania while he and CeCe were engaged, which was not a choice CeCe had wanted to make. Being of the southern persuasion, CeCe preferred any location below the snow line. However, Mike felt comfortable living near his mother's home, where he grew up. Her values of living life simply without airs, working hard, and not judging others were essential to him. Michael strived for success through hard work and remembered to look to God for the answers to decisions. He tried to do that each day. His new bride had received the keys to her home without complaint, but he knew she longed for white sneakers, not bulky-lined boots, a warmer climate, not snow on the drive, and a girl's night out at the theater, not an afternoon at the library each Tuesday. Because of her willingness to accept their new home, Michael brought CeCe to Savannah for their first anniversary. Michael's mother used to tell him how beautiful it was along the Georgia and South Carolina coast. His mother said she loved hearing the soothing tones of the shoreline coming in as she walked along the ancient mariner forest. Michael and CeCe could be with each other with minimal worldly distractions. They could enjoy their love for each other and share the more profound thoughts lost in the daily hustle and bustle.

Before flying home, the couple's last day on the coast was in Savannah. They held their room for an extra day to have more time on Sunday to enjoy the local vibe, freshen up between activities, and leave on a flight later in the day. CeCe had found a church on a square she wanted to attend. Mike did not refuse her. It was close to the bed-and-breakfast where they were staying. CeCe held Michael's hand as they entered the church that morning. The wind kicked up, and Michael adjusted his body to shield his wife from the draft. He accidentally touched something, and for a moment, he thought he recalled something that someone told him once in a story. He kept it to himself. Then they sat near the back of the church, near the center aisle. Mike looked around and saw the stone walls and wooden pews. It took him back in time. Many old buildings in Savannah had stories to tell.

Michael put his arm around CeCe and whispered something in her ear. Without saying a word or making an expression, she moved her purse between them and intently kept listening to the service. Following the service, Michael and CeCe walked down the street to the old coastal city. A host of complex emotions welled up inside Michael. The couple strolled, enveloped in the beauty of the draping Spanish moss-covered trees and blooming azaleas. Lunch would bring them back to the reality that the weekend was winding down.

They chose a diner with a sidewalk table to savor the remaining hours in Savannah. Here they could connect and the city for a lasting memory of their love as a couple on their anniversary.

Reverend Howard waited until the church was empty before leaving his post at the back. Another Sunday service had ended. He felt that sense of loneliness that comes upon a person when the lights go off at the show's end. Reverend Howard took off his robes and turned back into Charley, the man. He frowned at that thought. He didn't want people to see him as a figure to worship. Being a pastor was a likable vocation if it allowed him to be of some benefit to others. He liked the analogy of a light post on a dark, wet night in Savannah. The streets could be slippery for many. But the streetlights helped make the trip easier to get home safely. He had many offers to dine with friends on Sunday. Knowing the pastor was not married, well-meaning church members often invited him to their homes for a meal or to join them at one of Savannah's great restaurants. Today, he had another plan. He wanted to find some time to be with the rest of the city. There's a city beyond the church that he served. There's a connection he needed to make. As he walked down the street in his casual wear, fewer people saw him as a pastor, and he became just an ordinary man.

Charley's favorite diner was just a few blocks away. It was a favorite spot to become lost among the sounds of busing tables and children crying to drown out any deep thoughts. He thought of enjoying an omelet and biscuit in peace. Instead, Charley pushed on the establishment's front door and felt something again. He didn't know what or why, but he knew something was stirring in his heart. He sensed something he hadn't felt in a very long time. A warmth radiated within, giving a comforting sensation like a gentle touch. He first felt it at the church entrance this morning before the 11:00 service and then again during his sermon. "Hello, Charley," the server greeted when she saw him stand by the hostess's podium.

Charley greeted the young server, taking him to the counter as if he had a reserved spot. Those around him greeted him warmly as he shared the greetings back. He sat quietly for a moment as the staff chattered around him. A touch on his shoulder grabbed Charley's attention.

A young man who was a stranger to Charley greeted him warmly. "Reverend Howard, we saw you came alone to the diner today. My wife and I visited your church this morning and would enjoy visiting you. We are from out of town and will leave later today. We would be honored if you shared a conversation and a meal with us."

Charley responded graciously to an offer to join a couple at their table. What made him accept, he wasn't sure. It was a connection he wanted to make, and he made it without speech or thought.

The couple hailed from Pennsylvania, a lovely couple that had spent a week traveling around the area. How fortunate he was to have had them visiting his church today. They explained how they had seen the church as they had driven to their accommodations the night before. Their love for historic churches made them drawn to hear the service today. Reverend Howard was so enamored by their warmth and general enthusiasm that he spoke with them for a significant length over lunch. The church number rang at least two times. However, Charley was so engaged that he felt free to ignore the calls and not spoil a delightful conversation. The conversation was light, yet meaningful in an emotionally attached way. However, the time for lunch needed to end. With a tremendous pull on his heart, he did not want to lose touch with this impressive young man and his wife.

Reverend Howard exchanged cards with the young man and requested he call on him again when he was in town. The young man shared his appreciation and said he would love to return in a few months, the next time, perhaps for a week. Then, he would help with some of the building's needs for the church. Charley graciously accepted the visit and left the couple each with a warm blessing. Then, he left their table and walked several blocks before checking his messages and returning to his car at the church.

Michael and CeCe sat quietly on the plane somewhere over the snow-tipped North Carolina mountains headed for Pittsburgh. Holding Mike's hand, she softly told Mike how wonderful this trip had been. He smiled back and kissed her on the cheek. "I'll never forget this anniversary, and I'll never forget you. I've been to Savannah many times, but I never saw the low marshland on the southern coast of Georgia or Savannah as I have seen it this weekend through your eyes. You gave me a vision of what my mother had seen and loved. Previously, I saw only litter, unending hours on projects that made no sense, and rundown neighborhoods," Michael said with softness in his eyes. "Savannah had been a city of loneliness and disconnect for me whenever I went there on business, more so there than anywhere else I traveled. However, it changed for me this weekend with you being with me. Your presence helped heal a lost piece of my heart this weekend. I found something I never knew, and now I can be at peace about it."

Charley returned to the church office on Tuesday morning. On his desk lay an envelope with a message. It said several attempts had been made to reach Reverend Howard on Sunday after church. The attached envelope had been left on the offering plate on Sunday, with the attention of Reverend Howard. Charley thought to himself. He remembered getting a call from the church after the service. Charley also recalled the voicemail message from later Sunday night. But he deferred the issue until Tuesday. Charley thought the envelope could wait until then. Sunday had been refreshing for the soul as he recalled the young couple he had spent time with at lunch. He longed for such a visit again, but that was silly, given their home was some place in Pennsylvania.

My home is right here in Georgia, Charley thought to himself and chuckled. However, that thought was challenged on Tuesday by tidings in an envelope marked by Reverend Charles Howard. Charley focused on an envelope on his desk. So, this is what the calls were about, he thought. Reverend Howard opened the envelope containing a check for $100,000 and a second sealed smaller envelope with paper and a business card. With that, Reverend Howard stopped and breathed in; obviously, one of the older families of the church's membership most likely wanted to give generously to the church, he thought. He picked up the business card, and a touch from within swept over his heart just as it had done a Sunday morning at the door. It had happened again during the service and then again at the diner. A portal to his heart burst open after years of being tightly sealed. He could barely contain all that rolled out from inside. He had accepted his responsibilities over the years in so many ways. Reverend Howard had given his all to living a life prescribed to him by life's realities. Charley placed the card on his desk. He then reached into his jacket for a second card he had held in his pocket since Sunday. He carefully opened the folded white stationery that had carried the business card and check. The cards matched.

The memories floated back to the days when he

was young. He saw the face of an angel with tears of anguish, knowing she did not fit the family's expectations. How long had it been since he last felt that touch? He read the message on the folded paper, knowing its connection now. The conflict of a selfless love vs. selfish life was a topic for Charley to scrutinize further, but it was too overwhelming of a discussion now. As he sat and pondered the revelation for some time, a covering in his eyes was loosened. Charley traced the words on the note. Then, moving his lips and releasing the rush of air deeper than and more powerful than his larynx could hold back, he said the words that opened the locks of chains that had closed off a room of his heart for years. The card's handwritten message read: *Your son, Michael.*

t

Chapter 2

EIGHT MONTHS LATER AFTER the revelation that he had a grown son, Charley was making a trip. He left his home on one of the barrier islands that separated the downtown area of Savannah from the Atlantic Ocean. The destination was a tiny farming community in Pennsylvania, a place Charley would have never known existed or ever thought to spend a holiday with a son a year ago. He pondered some thoughts that he had been meditating on in his heart. I want people to understand something I have learned in my older years. I don't believe having a physical relationship outside of marriage is right. I have no right to judge, so I can't place that conviction on someone else. *God had it right all along, Charley thought.* It's for our good. It doesn't mean one loves that person less. Perhaps one loves them more when one waits and follows what God would have done rather than what the world says is okay. With maturity, practicing love helps us understand a deeper meaning.

Charley trusted God to bring people into our lives to help us live, heal our wounds, and understand us. My son has reached out to me to me with acceptance, and I want to do what's right for him. He deserves that. He took several steps over to the window and stared into the evening. The light from the lighthouse blinded him for a few seconds, and he turned to look away. Just as he turned, a box was illuminated in the closet. Charley walked over and tenderly lifted the box that had sat on the shelf unbothered for years. It was the last thing Ali gave him before she left. He had retrieved it from the trash after his mother had cleaned his apartment, removing any physical memory of Ali. Charley locked her memory farther into the depths of his soul, where no one looked, and no one could find her, not even Charley. He had accepted his fate of going on to seminary as his family wished. Charley would return to his father's church just as it should in the eyes of his parents. As he gently unfolded the pages, his fingertips grazed over each page. Charley reached for his glasses and sat to read the story Ali had left him; the last holiday they were together. It was her present to him that Christmas, along with a golden hair pup. She wrote on the card. Is there love in your tank for this little guy? All he needs is a little food, water, and walks by the sea. Charley closed his eyes for just a moment. That pup ran away while his parents watched it while Charley was away on a mission trip. Charley never replaced him, and he never said another word about the dog. Like Ali, it had vanished from his life, leaving space within. Charley pulled down the manilla envelope from his closet. The envelope appeared illuminated by the light from outside. He began to read the rough draft to himself as he sat on the edge of the bed. As he read to another room in his soul, his mind began to drift. Charley had compartmentalized away from conscious thought for so many years. The story began.

The innkeeper closed his eyes, but his mind was alert as he sat quietly in his private quarters at the back of the inn. Benjamin stroked the hand-painted miniature of a young woman, such a delicate image in contrast to his large hands scarred from years of sawing trees and placing fence posts as the pangs of grief knocked on the older man's heart. He rose from his chair to put the locket back when he heard the clambering of a coach drawing near. It was Christmas Eve, and the innkeeper was expecting one last guest.

"A special guest was coming," said the rider, who arrived late in the afternoon. The stranger had given no further details. Instead, he graciously accepted a small parcel of baked muffins and lifted himself onto the saddle of a tall chestnut. He directed the animal westward to meet the wagon trail.

Benjamin pondered. Who would come this way on Christmas Eve? From the window, he watched as more than one visitor ascended the steps to the porch. The visitors seemed important, but the meaning eluded the innkeeper as he greeted the guests as they entered.

Benjamin guided them to the enormous stone fireplace, where a fire was blazing. Hot beverages were brought out on a tray and served by the housekeeper. The quietness of the group was a sign of a secret between them. One man stood by the hearth while the other two travelers took chairs by the fire. Benjamin noted the two tall men's groomed hair and fashionable clothes. However, the scarred hands of the man standing by the hearth revealed he was not ignorant of hard labor. Benjamin took steps away from the warmth of the fire.

The traveler spoke out. "I sent a man ahead. We hoped our arrival was not unexpected," said the man standing by the fire. "We would like to warm up and talk with you. Please come." The man then patted the back of the vacant chair.

"Yes, a rider came before dusk," Benjamin replied. "I hope we can make you comfortable. We had three other parties this night, with a mother and young son sharing the same room. Another gentleman has a second room. I have two more rooms upstairs for guests and a third smaller room on the third floor that would be comfortable for the night. I run a simple inn with just the housekeeper and myself. Because we knew of your coming, the housekeeper kept something warm in the kitchen. Let me call Maeve to find out what she has ready this evening."

The tallest of the three visitors, already occupying a chair, stretched his long legs. "Sir, we are happy with your hospitality, but we don't wish to bring you extra *work tonight. I am most happy with this mug of hot cider. We were well prepared when we set out this morning. Please sit with us."*

Benjamin responded, "Yes, as you wish."

The same man continued in a cheerful voice. "I knew of your inn. Others passing this way have spoken of your hospitality and generosity. I know you have fed at least one hungry, orphaned child who wandered upon your establishment about twenty years ago. You found a dirty urchin up in the hayloft early in the morning."

Benjamin thought for a moment. "I vaguely remember an encounter with a tall, skinny boy who curled up in the hay in the barn. It's a wonder he didn't get critter bites all over him. I wanted him to stay longer after Mauve fed him breakfast. I would have found an excellent family to take him in, but he ran off with a wagon that had stopped the next day." Benjamin looked at the man closely and back to the fire with a slight grin. "Are you the young fellow who snuck into my barn that night?" Moisture filled the rim of the innkeeper's eyes. "To think you've come back to visit this old man? And that you remember the establishment between here and there that I feel honored," Benjamin responded as he drew his handkerchief from his pocket.

The housekeeper laid down the tray on the closest table and cried out. "Pardon me, but I could not help overhearing. I can't believe I'm seeing that scamp of a boy that ate six of my biscuits that morning. Such a handsome man you've grown to be!"

The man blushed from the attention he was receiving and opened his arms wide for the impending hug. "Those were the best biscuits and blackberry jam I have ever tasted," the man said. "Everything is as I remembered it." He looked at Benjamin and continued. "I have carried the gift you gave me right here," as he pointed to his heart and sniffed. My name is Samuel. Samuel Bennett."

"Well, what a Christmas Eve this has become!" Benjamin proclaimed as he pressed his hands together. The innkeeper then looked at the third passenger, a boy of less than ten years of age, sitting to the left of Samuel. "Would this be your son?"

The man standing at the hearth turned around with unexpected emotion. "No! Micah is my son." The man took another step closer, but then paused and looked away.

Benjamin looked at the young boy next to Samuel and smiled. "How fortunate you are. I hope this trip has been pleasant." Benjamin looked around the room, making eye contact with each guest and searching for clues about what would bring them to this ridge on Christmas Eve.

The boy showed an eagerness to speak. "Yes, we wanted to find the inn. We wanted..."

The boy's father held up his scarred and calloused

hand behind his back and signaled silence. His son immediately stopped mid-sentence.

Benjamin looked around at the three travelers quizzically. "I believe there is another secret here in this room, isn't there?"

The man standing alone walked to the back of the chair where the innkeeper sat. "Please, tell us how you come to be here."

Benjamin took a deep breath. "I came here thirty years ago. I brought my most precious treasures in life, my wife and my son." Benjamin stopped there and turned somber. "It is not a tale for Christmas Eve, my friend, when we should share joy and celebration."

"Please, I would like to hear what has kept you here these many years," said the man with a neatly trimmed beard, walking behind the innkeeper's chair.

The innkeeper pondered for a moment. Should this traveler's secret be so vital that Benjamin must tell of his own heart's emptiness? He took a deep breath and began. "I lost my family in an Indian raid while I was away buying supplies at the trading post. There were no traces of their bodies, only footprints for some distance. I searched for months, looking for them. I thought about ending my life after that dreadful day. My heart could not abandon their memory here in the wilderness, knowing that Annie and Matthew might still be out there. I lost trust in God. The bitterness in my heart wanted to grow and suffocate the good in me. One night I imagined myself walking along a path and seeing the light from a traveler's rest. It gave me hope and some peace. I began converting the house into an inn. I gave a piece of my heart to act as a beacon for anyone who stopped here. The light would guide them back to me if they passed my wife or son anywhere along their journey."

The man behind the innkeeper's chair caressed Benjamin's shoulders. "I am Matthew, Father. I found your light!" as he cried openly. "I am here. I found you in so many people, but it took Samuel to give me hope. The little boy from the loft grew up. Our journeys became entwined. Eventually, our partnership exposed missing pieces from my life. He put the pieces together of where my birth father might be after all these years. It was Samuel's idea to make this trip. I have a family. My wife and youngest son arrived earlier today. My father-in-law was the gentleman who traveled in their coach. I sent them ahead. The runner came back to tell me they had arrived safely. I followed behind to put things right in my head and heart. I, too, searched. Finally, my body was bundled up and taken away on the rump of a horse and rider. I was separated and alone from my family. I do not remember the first few years well. Eventually, I ran away into the wilderness. I met many people along the way, some good and some bad. I kept searching. I found my wife's father, who was a good man. I later met Samuel, a business partner, and a brother in spirit."

As Benjamin wept, he heard feet scamper across

the wooden floor. As the copper-haired child ran towards his father's pant leg, Benjamin saw a glimmer of a vision he had longed to behold for many years. He scooped the small child in his arms and hugged him tightly.

The boy raised his head from his grandfather's neck and peered outside the window. "There's the star, Daddy! It followed us here like you said it would."

"Yes, sweet one." Mathew followed his son's gaze to the shining star that glowed brighter than all the rest. "It followed us here on purpose, I believe."

Samuel moved from his chair and stood on the other side of Benjamin, bringing Micah with him to join those peering out at the evening stars.

By Ali Taylor

Charley folded the story and put it in his luggage. He zipped the bag. His emotions ran deep to where only one's soul and creator communicate. Finally, he settled into sleep, eager to set off on a trip to discover unknowns. He was scared, he admitted to himself, like the feeling of a hiker eating a candy bar and surprised by a bear on a hike while standing in chest-high willows. *Will I be eaten up and my life lost forever as I know it? But for the love of a son, I will not hide from others' scrutiny or run from overwhelming emotions*

Chapter 3

MICHAEL'S BARN WAS NOT what you might expect. A large barn in a meadow on the saddle of a mountain ridge welcomed the morning sunlight in the east and allowed for spectacular sunset views from the back porch. Even more hauntingly beautiful were the stars on a clear night. One could visualize American Indians still hunting for game and bedding down for the night along the ancient warrior paths. Reverend Howard walked downstairs to be greeted by CeCe's parents, who had gotten in yesterday but were staying in their RV.

"My daughter has a place right here for you, Reverend. Michael's gone out early. He said he wanted to check on something. He's working on something, as always, so we are left to hold down the fort and keep things running. I, for one, would be happy to go hunting in those woods, but my wife and CeCe forbid me to get close to any two or four-legged creature with a shotgun. They say it's because they don't believe in owning guns, including those for hunting."

"No, Richard. It's likely more your aim that they have serious concerns about," Michael said as he came up from the basement.

"Well, that too."

They all laughed while Michael poured himself a cup of coffee. "Now, Richard, how many stories have you told Charles since he's been up?"

"Not a peep from me. I figure I have to know the man first, and then I will be sure I can trust him with my honest confessions, at least as I recall them."

"Charles, Richard will tell you some long stories if you let him, and only half is the truth. It's always the challenge to figure out which half because all of it usually sounds like bull." Michael responded.

"Now, Michael, have I ever told you something that wasn't right?" Richard asked with a twinkle in his eye, knowing he had opened any possible previous escapades.

Michael quickly took Richard up on that challenge. "Oh, like the night I brought CeCe home when we were dating, and you gave me directions on how to get back to the interstate. That took me an extra hour and a half when it should have been fifteen minutes, tops."

"I just wanted to test your mantel a little, son. I figured that if you loved my daughter enough, you'd call on her again after showing that she was worth going the extra few miles. And, if you didn't call on her after going the long route over the old swamp road, then you weren't worth your salt," teased Richard, and then he turned toward Charley.

"Believe me, Reverend, you can't make some stuff up. Life happens. Now, you are from Savanah, CeCe tells me. I've been there, but never to relax. I hear the food and golf are excellent around that area." Richard turned toward CeCe and his wife and continued. "Your mother and I should make a trip there some time, CeCe. Maybe we could all go on a family trip."

"Richard, you can take me to Savannah any time you wish," as CeCe's mother kissed her husband's bold head. "You heard him, CeCe!"

"I meant when I retired. A man has to work to pay for all the groceries now and then."

"Yes, Love, and gas for all your toys that need to be stored somewhere as the homeowner's association won't let us park them all on the front lawn."

"Now, that's another thing!" Richard commented with exasperation, his hands flying up in the air and his eyes rolling upward.

Michael interjected, "Okay. I know it's time to get Richard in the truck and cut a tree on the back acreage, or his blood pressure will be all over the place today. I would bet that Charles is not a man that uses profanity, and I'm not going to be the one to guarantee that he will be free of corruption if exposed to my father-in-law if we continue the merits of home association covenants. It's something about those dos and don'ts list that causes flames in Richard's belly," Michael said.

"You wait, Michael, one of these days, when you are as wise as your father-in-law, you'll understand." Richard smiled mischievously.

Michael grabbed another sweet roll from the plate and looked at CeCe. "Share?"

"Not me. I won't be able to fit in my dress for this evening, and I've been working on it for three weeks," CeCe teased back.

"Well, in that case, you keep working on looking beautiful, and I will keep working on being sweeter." Michael smiled as he finished the last bite of a cinnamon roll in his hand. "Charles, why don't you come with Richard and me, and we'll get out of the ladies' way for a few hours? CeCe and Rona have some girl stuff to do before this evening. It always seems to require a charge card and a few lost hours in secret when they are together. Oh yeah, we will be back by four to be ready to go out for dinner."

Michael's father finished his toast and coffee and grabbed his jacket to follow the men. There was a sense of something warm inside his belly, and he was sure it wasn't the coffee. Is it supposed to be so comfortable around those he hardly knew? Just being accepted as part of the group was comforting. Charley turned toward the gathering of people. "I'm following the fellows, ladies. I don't know if it's the safest plan, but I suspect I am needed to keep somebody out of trouble. By the way, please call me Charley; Charles is for the days I wear a suit or robes. I liked to be called Charley when I am around friends and family."

"Well, that sounds fine, Charley. I will tell you a little secret about me. I am one to say what I think, which is quite a lot on some subjects. Sometimes I am salty with my words, like a hot sauce. It is good on everything and brings great flavor, but too much, and I can pollute the gumbo, so my family tells me."

"Charley, it is okay. Don't worry about Richard here. He's the best at what he does," Michael said as he grabbed his coat.

"And what is that?" Richard asked.

"We haven't quite figured that out yet, but we know you're good at something because we love you whenever you're around?" Michael teased.

"Well, it must be true because Rona has said that for years! Let's go, or the girls will find something for us to do, and I guarantee we won't like it," Richard said. The men started out the back door.

"How many miles do you have on this thing now, Michael?" Charley asked while he watched tuffs of seat stuffing ooze out of a seam with every bump.

"It's just over 303,000. However, I'm not putting this beauty to pasture until the truck drops," Michael stated proudly.

"Good thing we are heading towards the pasture and not the highway," Richard interjected into the conversation with amusement.

"The truck has been a great work machine," Michael responded as he turned toward Charley. "I usually don't drive it off the farm. However, my work partner has warned me that if parked off the property, he will call a tow truck and have it hauled away to an unknown location."

"I can't understand why he would say such a thing," Richard mumbled sarcastically. He then got busy reattaching the radio knob that had fallen off when the doors to the truck shut.

Charley enjoyed the banter between these two men. They had already formed a relationship that was more than a casual tolerance for one another. He wondered if he could connect this way with his son in time. How does one relate to an adult son when you were not there for much of his life? Charley just wanted to be himself, and he revolted from the thoughts of being pretentious to anyone, including Michael and his successful father-in-law. Richard was quick with his wit.

But Charley observed that CeCe's dad was no slacker regarding instinct and cunning. What would Michael think of his father? Charley understood the complexity of intertwining human beings in forming a relationship. He was a patient man. Trusting God and letting it happen is okay. It seemed more complicated now than it did the first time they met. Perhaps it was the vulnerability of letting someone get closer to the heart when the stakes were higher. No one can control the outcome.

Michael looked back at Charley in the rearview mirror. He knew he had made the right decision. "Charley, I think you're a good luck charm. Look at the perfect tree right there to the right. I wanted to move it anyway, as it blocked the view of the gap in the mountain range when you come up over that rise. When I saw that as a kid, I knew I wanted to own this spot. I love being here in all four seasons. It never gets old."

Charley looked out at the knoll to the right. "Nice tree, pretty large though, too large for a living room. Where are you thinking of putting it?"

Richard looked back and turned back to Michael. He deflected the conversation by asking Charley a question. "If you don't mind answering, how did it feel when you found out about Michael?"

Charley grinned, making him look like a young man again with his intense, dark eyes. "It is an unsettling experience, even when it's a good thing, like when you fall in love or get a promotion requiring you to pick up everything and move. I felt a longing after I left Michael and CeCe that Sunday. There was a soulish hunger that was intense after they left. I found something that touched me profoundly and filled that emptiness. I found something dear to my heart when I met Michael in that loud, crowded diner. He touched my shoulder and asked me to sit with him and his wife. It may have been Michael's hand, but I also felt God's touch. You may not understand that."

Richard went silent. "I understand, Charley. I did not mean to put you on the spot, but you answered well. Michael is special to me; I suspect I will figure out why in a more important way as time goes by, but for now, I accept what my thick skin and heart will allow me to understand."

The truck was making it through the gate by three o'clock, a tree tied to the top three men with rosy cheeks and muddy feet. Mission accomplished with one stop to go. Richard and Charley were dropped back at the house. Michael made a wave and reversed the vehicle back down the drive.

"Where's he going?" Charley asked.

"He's just giving those watching out for the old truck a bit of a chase," said Richard. "I sure hope he keeps the heap below fifty miles per hour; otherwise, the rattling and rocking we heard might be from the last bolt holding it together. Michael's a great son-in-law, just like having a son of my own. I thought no man would be good enough for my CeCe, but Michael has been brought up well by his mother."

"Yes, I can see that I have discovered that I have a son in just a few months. It's still overwhelming what all that means. He'll make a great dad!"

Richard silently looked at Charley for a minute and then stuffed a piece of spearmint gum in his mouth.

When Charley looked back at him, Richard quickly blurted out, "I'm trying to quit smoking," but his lips pulled back in the silence as he turned his head away.

Christmas Eve was an evening of dining out and genuine good company this year. As Michael predicted, CeCe and Rona had done their best to keep themselves occupied while the men were away. Michael had placed a little plastic card into his wife's purse before the guys left to ensure they had enough funds for their shopping spree. They also enjoyed playing secret elves, delivering treasures to the least expecting people. Finally, when the afternoon came and left, they were ready to return home and prepare for the Christmas Eve dinner.

Promptly at six, all were shaved, showered, perfumed, and ornamented appropriately to their tastes. CeCe and Michael led Charley to their vehicle while Rona and Richard followed in CeCe's four-wheel drive. The cars headed to the closest tiny village on a ridge along the main road built before the intervention of asphalt and motorized vehicles. In the center of the town, was an old inn built on a large corner lot. Lights from within and lantern lights flooding the walkway and porch, gave the structure a stunning beauty during the holiday season.

Charley was a good sport, but this was the part of the trip he wondered about if he would become homesick for Savannah. His parents filled the memory of many of his Christmas celebrations. However, in the last several years, he devoted himself to something he could do at the church. A few years back, it had been bleak, so Charley opened the church on Christmas Eve and spent the evening sharing with wandering men and women who sought the church as a refuge or a warm spot to share coffee and commune with others. One of those nights, he still remembered spending the eve and wee hours of Christmas morning at a local hospital. At least it was a way to connect with other humans working miracles inside the building on a dark, wet, cold December night. Charley clearly remembered the moon shining so brightly from above that he could see a circle of light surrounding him while he waited for help. This Christmas Eve night marked another memorable Christmas Eve in Charley's life. He was genuinely thankful and interpreted it as proof that God knew of all the wishes he had stored in his heart, not audibly spoken.

Michael pulled the car into the parking lot of a two-story stone structure built in colonial times. Lights glowed from within, and lanterns flooded the walkway and porch with an ethereal quality, giving the entrance a stunning beauty during the holiday season. The garland wrapped around the railing and lanterns lined the path to guide guests to the front porch. People freely walked along the sidewalk in front. Some stopped and walked over to a tree placed on the front lawn to add an ornament, while others took pictures. Pet owners stooped down and took selfies with their pets. Families stood in front of the tree wearing matching sweaters.

From what Charley could tell by the activity outside, the inn seemed to be the centerpiece of community Christmas cheer. He followed Michael and CeCe's lead as they left the parked vehicles. He knew he had not been here before, yet the locals seemed familiar. "Do you come here often?" Charley asked. He looked around and enjoyed seeing the snowflakes glimmer under the lamppost light.

Michael turned to look at Charley and smiled. He said nothing, but he spun his head to hide his emotions.

CeCe squeezed her husband's hand and looked up at him with bright eyes. "Nice job on the tree!"

Charley caught the line and spun his head to the tree decorated on the front lawn. The tree with decorations and garland and people milling about. "That's the tree we cut down today! How did it get here?"

"Remember, I drove it over in the truck after I took

you and Richard back," Michael responded.

Richard came up behind Charley with all smiles as he pointed out the tree. "I think we picked the perfect one, don't you?"

Charley paused for a moment and looked closer. He then followed the guests, peeking back over his shoulder to observe the tree almost tripping over the lantern that lined the walkway. Charley reached with his gloved hand to touch the sign that showed the date construction ended on the inn. Before he could connect his thoughts, Michael ushered Charley inside. His senses came alive like an electrical current reaching the tungsten in a light bulb. A hostess waited and directed the group to the back parlor, which had a fireplace warming the room with logs on the fire. Chairs surrounded the hearth and around the table. Beverages and savory snacks were brought out and put on a small sideboard. An adjacent room held a dining table. Charley assumed the staff had specially prepared the room with its festive ambiance for this family get-together. In part, he was correct.

Richard broke the silence. "I, for one, am starving, and I am going to take one of these warm buttery biscuits while we are waiting. Yes, it will ruin my supper, but I will go down with a smile."

Michael chuckled. "You know Hazel makes them just for you."

Richard showed bliss on his face as he took the

first bite. "Hazel, I love that woman. However, I am glad she only makes them for me at Christmas because will take me twelve months to burn the lard off the six-pack I now have."

Rona chimed in, "Please, Richard, you promised me you would keep the weight off!" Rona looked up at everyone. "He was a bear for two years, losing those sixty pounds. So that he can drive women wild with his new physic!"

"That's right, but the only one that counts is you," said Richard as he squeezed Rona's hand.

"Smart man!" Rona smiled as she kissed Richard on the cheek.

Richard blushed and teased, "Now, Rona, not in front of the children!" Everyone laughed.

Charley caught the last bit of the interaction and laughed, but his thoughts took a step away from the present. He was sifting his mind with clues: the hearth, the lights along the path, an inn on a hill, and the smell of biscuits. Where have I heard or seen this scene before? As Charley tried to process it all, the hostess returned to the group and announced that dinner was ready to be served in the dining room. Charley followed the others when he glanced at a tall, elegant woman's reflection in the mirror. "Ali!" he said her name before he could hold it back.

"Michael, I hugged you earlier when you brought

the tree, so let me hug CeCe and her family." Ali came from around the table and over to the group. "I was lighting the candles. Will you light the other candle for me, Charley?" She smiled with a moistened tear in her eyes. She laid the box of matches in his hand and covered his hand with her own. "It's been a long time, but I am happy you found your way here. The inn is mine, and this is where we celebrate Christmas Eve. I wanted you to be here this year with us when I heard that you and Michael had found each other."

Charley stood in astonishment as Ali moved on to the other guests. "Rona, what have you been doing for this man? I hardly recognize him." She winked at Richard, who blushed.

"Ali, it's been nothing but green things and tree bark around our supper table," Richard remarked. "Tonight, I am making up for two years of veganism!"

"You look fabulous!" Ali moved over to squeeze his elbow.

"I'm finally carrying a six-pack, the first time since I was in college," Richard beamed. "You want to see?"

"No!" Michael burst in with a laugh. "I take him with me to be with my family and friends, and he will embarrass me every time!"

"Ah yes, I promised something about not embarrassing you," Richard chuckled.

Charley held on to the mantel before turning

around. His heart felt as if it pumped straight through his ribs. He wondered if his eyes would expose the stirring in his soul.

Michael spoke, "Since you don't need an introduction to anyone here, Charley, I will be the first to say that Mother and I wanted to have you all here this Christmas, and she insisted on having dinner at the inn. My mother owns and lives here. That's why we got the tree early today so we could bring it to the front lawn. It's a tradition here. You know, a tree, a sign of life and all that stuff. Mother enjoys the holidays here. The tree has become a beacon to those in this small town. People come from around the area on Christmas Eve and add ornaments to the tree. A Christmas globe from Japan hung one year when an exchange student staying with a family down the street stopped by. It's cool on Christmas Eve to watch people come by throughout the day and add something. Sometimes, they stop to take photos with their pets or children. It's extraordinary to watch every year."

Charley looked at the end of the table. "Yes, Ali always lit up her world with her love for life, even when I knew her in college. Charley smiled and looked into the eyes of the one he had lost years before. I remember she was fond of a specific plant around the holiday. Although I think it was illegal then."

"Now, Reverend!" Ali lit up with a smile. "I cannot tell a lie, but if I remember right, someone there knew the plant by its genospecies name and showed me how to roll the dry stuff in cigarette papers. I did not know what I was growing in my room. My roommate gave me the plant. I just kept watering it for her."

Rona chimed in with laughter. "I can already tell this will be an entertaining dinner party with everyone together."

Everyone settled in around the table for the meal. Charley said the blessing and the conversation easily flowed with the serving of succulent meats and side dishes of vegetables prepared to perfection and would make any experienced chef jealous.

"Yes indeed," Richard replied as he took a generous scoopful of oven-warmed yams smothered in marshmallow cream. Tomorrow, I'm back to eating tree bark. But tonight, I am going to enjoy it all!"

As dinner progressed, the conversation stayed light and entertaining. Richard was in his element of telling tall tales from his day-to-day life. CeCe and Michael found joy in knowing that this was a gathering of people who genuinely bonded with one another. Charley and Ali, in full grace, never faltered in speaking well of one another. What Ali felt, no one could tell. She was at her best as a witty hostess, and tonight she sparkled. As for Charley, he watched the interaction between dinner guests. He was older and wiser now and did not believe himself foolish enough to fall for a man's empty charm. Men are warriors at heart, tough to fight demons and break chains, but vulnerable to beauty. His eyes beheld the beauty, but the vulnerability was something even Charley would have a tough time facing after all these years. Life happens between the lines on paper.

Ali could see Charley's eyes pick up the flicker of the candle's flame. His large hands held the water goblet with tenderness, as if holding a sparrow. A thought came to her mind of the difference between humility and being timid. *Charley had grown in humility, but there was no shyness or tepidness about this man. Instead, an aura of quiet strength had developed since they were in college.*

As the evening ended, Michael threw his father the keys. "Come home when you like. We're going home." Richard and Rona followed the couple to the front door. "Mother, thank you for having us tonight," Michael said before he bent over to kiss his mother. "Save me some leftovers, preferably a piece of your German Chocolate cake, but I will be thankful for a slice of anything if you or Hazel made it."

Ali smiled. "You know I will bring over something, so CeCe will not need to cook for lunch or supper tomorrow. My treat."

The group walked down the lit sidewalk. CeCe reached into her handbag for a tissue when she felt something else in her purse. "Wait a minute. I have something here." She grabbed Michael's arm and pulled him over to the pine he had placed in the yard earlier. "I want to put it on the tree. Can you reach for a branch close to the top, Michael?" She handed him an orb that had a red and white petaled camellia. CeCe looked back at Ali and Charley. "It is from Michael and me from our trip to the coast."

Ali blew them a kiss. For the first time this evening, she wiped a tear from her cheek, revealing a glimmer of her thoughts while she stood and admired the ornament while shivering in the cool winter air. They waved back and scampered off to the car, where Rona and Charles were waiting. The car lights soon faded as the passengers traveled over the rise of the hill.

"You were an excellent parent to Michael, Ali. He has all the qualities one would want in a son. He is intelligent, kind, and articulate."

"Yes, he is beautiful on the inside and out. CeCe is the perfect wife for him. It was easy to let him go when the time was right, because I trusted that his heart would make the right choice. I think it has, don't you?"

"Yes, they are perfect together. CeCe's father adds spice to the family." Charley grinned.

"Oh," Ali said as she gently touched Charley's forearm. "You are bad!" she giggled. "Richard is a joy. He has a great big heart underneath his facade. He is also intelligent. Michael works for him. Did he tell you that? Michael has a lot of voice in the company and is a good partnership. Rona and Richard have another son who was permanently injured in an accident when he was younger. He and Michael have become close."

"That must be Stephen. I have heard Michael talk about CeCe's brother."

"Yes, I think he had other holiday plans, so Richard and Rona made the trip and are spending it here this year. They will leave shortly to go back. Michael can live here because they have a regional office not far away. He travels a lot despite working a lot from home." Ali directed Charley to come back inside and guided him to a small den to the right of the stairwell. Ali had decorated the room with comfortable chairs that were great for reading, a sizable maple-stained desk, and shelves filled with books and framed pictures. "I can look out the windows and watch the weather, or like tonight, I can see the tree's decorations and people along the street. I sit here and write most of my books. I even wrote the one about being lost in a Canyon right here. I've been to Arizona and Utah, but I wrote it mostly sitting here in my jeans, flannel shirt, and my favorite fuzzy socks," Ali said as she touched the desk's wooden surface. She looked over at Charley, trying to connect to the man who plopped himself down in the wingback chair next to the desk. Instead, Ali casually walked toward a corner, moved an ottoman, and placed it under Charley's legs and feet. "That should feel better," she said with a softness and warmth in her voice.

"I could sit like this and fall asleep easily," Charley said.

"I often do," Ali responded. "It's my favorite spot on the entire property."

"Do you remember the story you gave me about an inn just like this?" Charley asked. "I brought it with me from Savannah, thinking I would give it to Michael. I did not know this place even existed in real life."

"The inn has been here all this time. When I wrote the story, I did not know about the inn." Ali told him. "I bought it about five years ago. I briefly recall the story, but I don't have a copy. Charley, you have the only version that I know still exists. I was not a professional writer then. I believe Michael's conceiving occurred around the same time I wrote that story. It must have been a great story!" She smiled back with a blush. "Do you think you can make me copy?"

"Yes. I will make you a copy," Charley said with a serious undertone. "You know I cannot return to that same person I was then, Ali. I wouldn't have left it the way it ended if I had known you were pregnant. Life would have been different. Maybe we wouldn't have married, but I wouldn't have let you take care of a child without support. I wouldn't have left you with that responsibility alone."

"It is good to know that we both have become responsible people."

"Ali, I am who I am. Whatever mistakes I made on the way, I confess it all to the One above. I do not live with shame. I want to learn and be taught and be open to God more. I know I'm not going to be perfect."

"That is a trait I admire, Charley, humbleness. I dislike people who attempt to shame people because they didn't know better or made wrong choices. It's all in the learning process. I should have told you, but I just could not hurt you and your family by what our relationship meant to them. I would not let your parents take our child away from me, either. I was going to be the child's mother. I was going to be the best mother I could be because I loved that child and his father, too."

"Ali, you did a great job, and I am blessed to know him now after you've done the hard part of raising him." He's going to be a great parent because of you.

Charley glanced outside. "Do people stop by all night to look at the tree?"

"Yes," she replied. "It will slow down after 1:00 in the morning. People leave midnight mass and pass by on their way to their destination. A few people will trickle by through the night. They are closing many small churches in the smaller communities, so perhaps fewer people will stop by the inn in years to come. It's not a thriving area, but it's peaceful and simple life here. I travel enough to give me stimulation."

"Do you feel wanted here, Ali?"

"Is that a trick question?" Ali looked at Charley, wandering for a moment. "I feel accepted here, which is important to me. I am always asking God where you want me to be. I have not always gotten an answer that I can hear. I get to be near Michael and CeCe, but I suspect they made their home in the area to stay close to me. However, I want them to be where they are supposed to be, and I don't want them to feel anchored. They are still young. I do not feel like I am describing my life as the adventure that it has been. I am pleasantly content here, Charley."

"Ali, you are still the beautiful person I remember you to be. That's beyond what I think of you as a mother. Michael is an example of what you gave him."

"Michael's a part of you too, Charley. As I watched him grow, he had so many of your attributes. Michael likes only black bath towels. He puts a bit of cinnamon in his coffee, and as you found out earlier, his favorite dessert is German Chocolate cake, but typically only when baked at home. I used a recipe you told me once that tasted like your mother's and was your favorite. I never told him."

Charley took Ali's hand. "I can't agree with some of our decisions back then. But this is now. I am proud of you for what you have accomplished. Ali, you have done well."

"Thank you. I've made peace with many things." Ali smiled and showed a genuine countenance of peace that was a gift as much as her words. "So, what about you, Charley? You were always refined, well-studied, well-groomed, and never missed your mark. What are things like for you in Savannah?" Ali asked.

"I am happy, or at least content. Between my grandparents and parents, the money they left me was enough that I could have left and moved on. I felt I needed to be where I was. Although lately, I have longed for something. Not a change, really. I want... to feel alive." Charley wanted to put it in the right words to help her understand. "I'm hungry for something, Ali, and I don't know what it is. I've been faithful to doing God's work, but I feel a longing. My head says that's a sign of digging deeper into knowing God, but I'm unsure how to apply that in my life. Look at you. You write and have this great inn that you have as a business and a home. You've raised Michael. That's wonderful, and you have something to show for your efforts. I provide ministry to a beautiful, broken city. I can't fix all the needs. That frustrates me. It's never going to be a perfect world."

"I haven't been to your specific church, but I know you have a genuine love for people more than I do." Ali looked at him tenderly. "I love people from a distance. They take so much from me, but you're not like me. You love to be around people. People naturally come to you. You have something that they want. It's uncanny the way people are attracted to you."

"I'm not sure what that could be. I could say the church answer," Charley shrugged, then continued. "I'm just me."

"Do you know how much I missed being with you? Our conversations brought something refreshing to my life that seemed dull. You lured me with your charm," Ali responded to Charley without hesitation.

"That's hard to believe," Charley softly spoke with a grin. "Oh, was it our first date playing racquetball, and I gave you a good shiner? Let me think some more. Oh yeah! It must have been love when you shared hash browns fried and spiked with paprika, green peppers, and onions on a game day at the diner next to the campus gate. I recall kissing you with all that onion in my breath on the way back to the field. I must have been a poster of the hunk of the year for the sorority set on that day."

"I always shared my breath mints with you first," Ali giggled. "I would close my eyes and listen to you talk about physics back then, and it would make me believe I loved physics. You influenced me to take that course, and I almost did not pass it. Maybe I should have realized that your influence was not always good for me." Ali smiled with a twinkle in her eyes.

Charley bantered back. "But you passed the course with my influence, so I must have had some positive purpose for my life back then. Besides, you had a lot of friends. You were just more selective about what you did with your time and the friends you kept. Instead, I spent time with anybody who would let me hang around."

Ali smiled as she visualized scenes long forgotten. "You spent time with some interesting characters back then. I don't know if that was true of your friends in Savannah, but that was undeniably true in your dorm and when we hung out together in the evenings."

"The only female friend I brought home to my parents' place while I was in college was you," Charley said as he stared back at Ali. Charley paused for a moment. "I'm going to be here for just a couple more days. I want to spend some time with you if you allow me."

"Me?" Ali had a playful, surprised look on her face.

"Yes, if you go up and change. I will promise to be a gentleman and sit here and enjoy the view from the window."

"Okay. I will be back in five minutes." Ali then rushed out of the room.

"I'm not counting, but five minutes sounds just about right, or you will miss the carolers coming this way several blocks down."

"Don't let them go before I'm back!" Ali yelled back from down the hall.

"Okay." Charles laughed. It felt like he was a twenty-year-old waiting for Ali to come down from her all-girls dorm. There was never this fear or anxiety or internal drama. It just happened. She would come down with her freshly pressed jeans and a simple shirt or sweater. They would go to the library or go off for a walk. Sometimes they would walk around the lake. Sometimes there would be an activity at a non-denominational church just beyond the university's gates. They loved music, and Ali was talented at singing and playing the flute. She had introduced him to jazz and classical composition. Charley introduced her to the sounds of guitars and percussion. Ali liked it when he played his music for her. Charles felt the pleasure in Ali sharing her interest with a piece of his heart.

While Ali was gone, he let his mind go back to many years ago when he brought Ali to his home for the holidays and the end of the school year. Ali had no family to go back to except for two aging grandparents. Charley's family was very much intact and part of his life in every way possible. They had a plan for his future. When Ali left mysteriously during her stay with him at his parents' home, he never saw her again. No word and no message. His parents determined his future.

"How does this look for a middle-aged woman who eats vegetables three times a day? I have not eaten pizza in seven years," Ali said with teasing in her voice.

"You look stunning, even in jeans. As for pizza, do not look at me to put temptation your way. Whatever you are doing, you are doing something right to keep yourself looking healthy and young. You should bottle and sell it as an over-the-counter remedy for about everything," Charley responded with a smile.

"Thank you. I will take that as a compliment." Ali

pulled on a knitted toboggan and matching gloves. "Come on. Let's meet up the people on the sidewalk waiting for the carolers to pass the inn. I want to sing tonight." She grabbed a basket on the way out. "Oh, you can still play, can't you?" Ali questioned Charley as she opened a closet door.

Charley grabbed the guitar case from her. "What's this about?" Charley asked.

"You'll see," Ali said. She winked back at him as she reached the front door.

Ali showed Charley a place where they could await the carolers. A couple of benches sat in front of the inn under the wooden marquee. The lamp post illuminated the area. "Let's sit down there and see if we know they're singing music."

"Merry Christmas," said the man in the group's center as they began their rendition of a popular Christmas Carol. Charley followed the group's tempo on the guitar and continued for a few more songs. Ali then asked if she could sing her favorite song, and as she did, Charley watched as she floated within the group, passing out wrapped gingerbread cookies with red and green ribbons to all who circled the group. They responded with appreciation, and the group slowly moved up.

Charley sat and put the guitar back in the case. "You have this magic!"

She touched his shoulder to dust off a snowflake. "I don't make magic, Charley, but I have faith in something some may not understand. But Charley, you have the gift of helping people understand. Even playing music provides clarity to the meaning of the lyrics. You always had that skill."

Charley laughed, "I am surprised my fingers are still nimble enough to play. I have not done it in a while. Do you play now?" pointing to the guitar case.

"No, it's Michael's old guitar. We bring it to the dining room or the porch if we have someone to play it for us. Michael will sometimes play it for enjoyment. He knows every song of your favorite artist."

"No, sir!" Charley smiled in shock. "Who taught him those songs?"

"He's listened to a few growing up. I played many types of music when he was a child. Therefore, he developed a general fondness for all kinds of genres. Michael has a raw talent for music composition and performance if he ever wanted to develop it."

"Well, let's take this back in. It's getting late, and I'm sure you are tired, but would you mind staying up longer? Maybe I could help you with something. Are you open on Christmas?"

"No. Christmas is the only holiday we are closed. I don't have any overnight guests checking in on Christmas Eve. Instead, I have my family dinner late on Christmas Eve. That allows the inn to be open for breakfast, brunch, and a special lunch menu, with the last seating at two. We try to have everything put away by six. I usually let everyone go home, and my family and guest have dinner at seven. Hazel, the hostess at the door, is a friend who helps and sometimes joins us fur dinner. She wanted to go home and wait for her first grandchild to enter this world, and Hazel finally got word shortly after you arrived. That lovely lady makes the best biscuits if I must brag about her myself. She makes the cookies too, but this is my grandmother's recipe, as Ali pointed to the remaining cookie in the basket. I always get the first bite when she makes these to know if it tastes authentic, as I remember them as a child."

"Are there any more left that you could add to the slice of chocolate cake you're saving for Michael?" Charley asked with a grin. "I am too full right now. But tomorrow evening, I think I will crave for one of those while I read a book," Charley said.

"Well, it just happens. I might take a tin full of cookies over in the morning, along with Michael and CeCe's Christmas present."

"So, what did you get them? Oh, maybe I should take that back. That seems rather out of place."

"It's okay. I don't mind. I bought Michael and CeCe a pair of kayaks."

"You are kidding me! I would love that as a gift! Do

they go out on the river much?"

"Not really. Michael and CeCe both work and don't have much time to spend together. He enjoyed going on a day trip with a friend this past year and could not stop talking about it. He had his camera attached to make a video of him going over the rapids down a West Virginia river. While you are here, ask him for a link or have him play it for you on his computer. He is talented in many areas. The only thing I can think of that he doesn't like to do is write. He did not take that after you. However, if forced, Michael can write something concise, direct, and in perfect form."

Charley recalled Ali's free spirit and asked, "Do you go away from the inn much?"

"Yes, I have people who will care for things if I go away for a few days. However, I dislike being away more than a week." Ali responded. "I have capable people that work with me as needed. I've worked out contingency plans for most things. But the surprise events happen, and you have to go with the flow, right?"

"I'm hearing a pretty confident lady here. You've developed into a businesswoman, a mother, and a community member. Is there anything that you have failed at doing?

She laughed. "Oh yes! There are lots of things I'm not good at doing. I've learned to avoid them. For instance, you will never see me float on one of a fiberglass board down a river. I can't swim, and I don't want to learn. I'm not a great speller, but I use my tools on the computer to help me. My proofreading skills are deplorable. I fail at things, and I learn from that failure. I try to keep it to a minimum if I can help."

"Did you ever date anyone seriously through the years?" Charley asked.

Ali cringed at that. "I guess that is something I'm not very good at, either. I can't flirt."

"That is not true, as you are doing a pretty good job right now," Charley teased with a smile.

"I'm the person I am," Ali said, then paused. "They must not let you out of the church much in Savannah!"

Charley laughed. "Believe me. There's enough that goes on around spins around me in my world. I need to wear blinders most of the time. It's a crazy world out there. I try not to be corrupted by all the stuff out there. But life has many positive and negative experiences, and I live in the world."

Ali looked away for a moment of sadness in her eyes. Her thoughts wandered back to another place where garland wrapped the streetlights and camellias bloomed on front lawns. The door to a dungeon of her soul cracked open. Feeling the remnants of an old wound like a glacier melting away on a mountain peak, Ali took a moment to process what she was feeling. She stopped to honor that inner part of herself that only a few were ever let in. Ali looked into his dark eyes, which sparkled in the light. "Charley, was I corrupting to you? I didn't mean to say that. I don't want to say things now that have been forgiven and put away. It's Christmas. Michael invited you here as his quest and as a part of his family, and I want you to be a part of his life if he wants that in his heart. There's no water on the bridge."

"Ali, we made mistakes, which is a part of growing up and maturing into who we are to become. Others may influence us, but we make that final decision. I can't always correct the choices, but I can move forward. Sometimes I'm allowed to be an instrument of healing. Other times, I have nothing to offer to fix what has happened. My faith says I will turn it over to a perfect love. I am not."

"Well, Reverend Howard, I think I just went to church," Ali responded.

Charley looked down at his hands and then back to Ali's dark, doe-like eyes. "It is my way. I am sorry. I do not want to lecture anyone, even during Sunday services. If I can share a piece of my heart with a group of other travelers, and they can do something with me, then great. If it does not grow, I go on. I can't control how the words will grow. I just threw them out there. I'm kind of like Richard in that way. It just comes out."

Ali laughed. "I see the likeness."

Charley allowed a few moments of silence before

he posed a more tender question to a heart that had carried a great deal. "How have I hurt you? You walked away and kept me from knowing about Michael. When you said you feared my family would have taken him away, I heard you. But, Ali, do you think I would have taken Michael away from you when I saw how much you loved him? I'm not that ugly of a person."

Ali shook her head. "No, you were never that kind of person."

"Did you think somebody would punish you and take Michael away?"

"Charley, I take responsibility for my choices. Let's leave it at that."

"I want to understand, Ali, so that I can honor that part of you. I would have been scared. Did something occur to keep you from telling me?" Ali remained quiet.

"Did something make you run away from our relationship after coming to Savannah?" Charley probed with a gentle voice. He wanted honesty.

Ali remained silent, but tears started flowing down her cheeks from her closed eyes."

"Ali, I am sorry. I don't think those tears are just sadness, are they? I know you enough to cry in silence like this when you are angry."

Ali struggled to hold back more tears.

Charley pushed a little further on a topic that was

very dear to him. "Ali, please let it out and let it go. It's safe now. The people who hurt you are gone now, aren't they?"

Ali nodded her head affirmatively.

"Someone in my family told you a lie. The truth of my heart's intentions was never heard or conveyed to you. I apologize for the ignorance and ugliness of that person's heart that caused you to run. Ali, I have said, and I will repeat it. You were special. You have a heart that glows like a star in the sky. Your beauty is shown in the world you influence." Charley sat back in silence, allowing Ali to soak in the message for a moment. They continued to talk for some time, watching the evening stars and listening to the twilight sounds from the bench at the side entryway.

"Do you remember when we backpacked on one of those barrier islands south of Savannah? Back then, we were brave souls. I do not think I would have it in me anymore with alligators and snakes. How did we not get eaten by the predators as midnight snacks?"

"You had your lucky charm with you," Charley responded as he teased her with his smile, dimpled chin, and widened eyes.

"I guess so!" Ali laughed.

"Believe me. I would have been a bigger powder puff than you if a snake had snuck in the tent or an alligator had called on us in the middle of the night.

Some warrior I would have been then if some night predator came along."

"Well, maybe, but I knew I was safe when I left my snacks in the car, and you shared your sandwich and even gave me your trail mix with chocolate-covered nuts." Ali smiled with her lips covered with light pink gloss, just like she wore it back then.

"I didn't know that's how females selected their future mates; I will keep that in mind the next time I have to give birds and bees talk to some of our teenagers at church. Ali, I will need to go home, and you will need to get some sleep. Can I help you with anything before I leave?" Charley asked.

"No, I am good. I will lock up and find my way back to the apartment."

"Goodnight, Ali. Thank you for dinner and for being my companion this evening. I wasn't expecting to play the old pick and strings, but it was worth every moment. I want to spend more time with you while I am here, although I will return in two days. I need to spend some time with Michael, too. Will you be here tomorrow evening?" Charley asked.

"I am planning to drive over to Michael's and CeCe's in the early evening to take over their presents."

"Perfect." Charley gave a brief hug to Ali and drove away out of sight before Ali walked into the inn. She held her back to the door with her eyes closed, storing the memory. Ali's mind was full of thoughts. She could not express them, but she could feel them providing comfort as a child held in the arms of a loved one.

Two hours later, CeCe nudged Michael while snuggled in a soft flannel blanket. "Is that Charley downstairs?" she asked in a whisper.

"Most probably," Michael mumbled under the covers, with his eyes still closed.

"Should we go down and check on him?" CeCe whispered.

"Probably not," Michael mumbled some more.

"He hasn't come upstairs yet," CeCe whispered again.

"He's a grown man, CeCe. I think he can take care of himself," Michael responded, while turning over and repositioning his pillow.

"Seeing your mother after all this time? That must have been a shock to him."

"Yes. I'm sure it was," Michael murmured as he curled closer to his wife.

"Aren't you curious about how things went?"

"After drinking a couple of your father's coffees made with the best whiskey, my thoughts have become a pleasant fog. However, in my more sober state of mind in the morning, I will be most interested in discovering what Charley is thinking. I am perfectly content to allow two adults to work through their life's story on their own, as they are both reasonable and kindhearted-natured people."

Across the yard inside the motor home, Richard and Rona were dancing to zydeco music to an old movie soundtrack in the dark. Richard's favorite scene involved a green stuffed alligator. Rona had put one in her luggage on their honeymoon. It became the "third wheel" and running joke in their photos from the trip to California. Over time, it just became a part of their romantic story.

Rona lifted her head from Richard's shoulder and asked, "What a lovely evening? Do you think Reverend Howard misses not being in Savannah this Christmas? There must be a lot at church this time of year."

Richard responded, "He is where he wants to be. But I will also say I think he is where he is supposed to be. Perhaps he has found a new purpose. That, my love, is a valuable gift." Rona nuzzled Richard's chin. "I think you may be right."

Ali was sitting in the wingback chair, the same chair that Charles had sat in just a few hours before. She took a sip of the coffee and closed her eyes, feeling the fabric's texture in her hands. There was a pleasure just sitting in this spot this morning, but what would it all mean in the bigger picture? Ali was a firm believer in faith to guide her way through life. Choices are part of understanding who I am becoming, she thought to herself. This joy in the morning was an excellent afterglow of the evening's events, but emotions were fickle friends. Ali mentally analyzed Charley's behavior yesterday and found herself attracted to too much of what she saw. She thought, Charley, you still win me over with your kindness and relaxed manner. He was pleasant and not judgmental. He appeared to listen intuitively. Ali was trying to process what it was like to visit Charley after all these years. Let me enjoy the moment, God. Thank you for this gift of friendship this Christmas.

Ali made it to the window and saw the street outside. Perhaps no snow today. But the sky was blue, and the sun glowed. She wandered to the inn's kitchen and began pulling things from cabinets. Scoops of glazed nuts were placed in bags and placed in green containers. Cookies packed in red ones were wrapped in gold ribbons and set on the counter. Ali breathed in the aroma of cinnamon and molasses in the air while she worked. It made her happy. It was one of the few memories she had of her grandmother that she wanted to cherish for the rest of her life. The inn gave her those feelings of home.

Charley had slept by the fireplace during the wee hours of Christmas morning. The warmth from the fire felt good, and the glow gave him a sense that he was not alone. Comforted by the heat and the crackling sounds of the wood, he felt alive. Christmas for Charley was a day of relationships. He never got sucked into the commercial trappings of the season. Charley knew he was a seeker at heart. He wondered what it all meant. Wisdom isn't always what one would expect. Sometimes it's even hidden. Charley eventually put out the fire and went to bed. He rested peacefully through the mid-hours of the morning, and when he finally awoke, he saw a new day shimmering through the glass panels of the window. *Charley thought today was the best Christmas morning of my life.* He stretched and looked out over the landscape. He heard the sounds below and saw the time on the clock. It was already midmorning, and everyone else's day had started. He quickly dressed and completed his morning routine. As his feet reached the last step, he heard muffled voices from the kitchen, so he ventured to that area.

"Just in time, Steven. Reverend Howard is here now," Richard said. "You can ask him yourself." He put the phone on speaker on the kitchen counter. "Charley, this is my son, Steven, and his fiancé. She's why he decided not to spend the holiday with us this year."

"Good morning, Reverend Howard. I am Steven, CeCe's brother. Michael and I have talked about your project in Savannah."

"Hello, Steven. I am enjoying sharing this Christmas with your family."

"Well, I am glad. It was good for my mom and dad to get away. Maggie and I have a question we would like to ask you. We were wondering if you would officiate at our wedding in April. And we would like to have a small ceremony at your church in Savannah."

"Steven, I would be honored. Is there a reason you would like to have the wedding in Savannah and not Louisiana?"

"Maggie and I have talked, and Savannah seemed to have more checks than some of the other choices," Steven answered the question honestly. Of course, several other factors were also part of the decision, but Reverend Howard did not need to know that.

"I am sure we can work together to make it happen," Charley responded.

"Great!" Michael said. "I think this is perfect. Well, Steven, I think we have done well this morning. We are sending your parents on their way tomorrow."

"Anything you want us to pack and send down to you?" CeCe asked.

"No, I think we are good."

"Okay, Steven. We'll talk with you as we start back," said Richard.

"Okay. Have a glorious holiday! Good to talk with you again, Reverend Howard." The screen went blank and everybody dispersed.

Charley pulled Michael away privately and asked, "What did he mean by that?"

Michael looked at Charley with a flat affect,

shrugged his shoulders up and down, and said, "I don't know."

Charley looked at Richard, but was halfway out the door with a bag of goodies. Charley followed behind to ask Richard the same question.

Richard just kept walking and said something that sounded like, "People meet all kinds of people. Sometimes they say things without thinking," and he walked away.

Richard's response did not convince Charley of a hidden message, but he stored it in his mind for now. After that, he would have the chance to talk with Steven again and hopefully decode the unknown parts.

Richard grabbed Charley's hand and shook it. "Thank you for accepting my son's request. It will mean a lot to all of us." Richard glanced over at his wife and winked. "Rona, I think someone heard us talking about a trip to Savannah. Michael's father arrived, and now we have our opportunity. I don't think I will be too good at driving the rig I have now. I'll trade it for a small sports car to weave in and out of traffic on the crowded streets. I might even make it a convertible."

Rona just shook her head. "He is impossible, you know, but to love this man is my purpose in life," Rona teased. "Some men mellow with age. Richard only became more surprising.

Michael took back the conversation and invited

Charley officially to join them for breakfast. "We have coffee ready, and there are plenty of things to choose from this morning, so make yourself at home and fix a plate. That's what we are like when we are all together on Christmas."

"Thank you. I will grab some coffee, and that's all I need for now," Charley commented as he went to the counter with cups and a coffee pot ready.

"Michael, I don't know your plans, but I would love for you to take me down to the barn. There has to be something I can help you with or do." Charley asked.

Michael looked at CeCe and smiled. "Yeah, there is something there. I want you to see what we are keeping there. I think everyone should come."

"We want to come! You've had the barn off-limits since we came," Richard responded. "Did you build a still there or something?"

"Dad," CeCe gently tapped her father's shoulder. "You know Michael wouldn't do that, but we have a great surprise!"

"You all get ready, and I will follow you down after I take a couple more sips of coffee," Charley said.

"No, we can wait. We had our breakfast in peace before Steven called. You deserve the same. Try a muffin. CeCe makes the cranberry walnut ones that are extra good," Michael requested by putting the basket in front of Charley.

"Okay, I will." Charley picked one out and took a bite. "Wow!" After taking another bite and washing it with pure black liquid goodness from his mug, Charley exclaimed. "This is excellent! Michael, you must eat well between your mother and CeCe!"

"I can't complain," Michael laughed. "Rona can compete with the best, too, despite what you may hear Richard say about eating tree bark and alien green stuff." Michael looked back at Richard and laughed.

"She only brings out the good stuff when we have guests!" Richard quipped. Rona gave Richard a pinch on the arm, and he gave her a peck of a kiss on the cheek.

"I'm ready," Charley said as he went to the hall closet to get his gloves and coat. "CeCe, are you going to let us in on the secret Michael has been hiding? Maybe a hint?"

CeCe laughed. "Not a peep from me." She linked her arm with Michael and headed out the back door. The rest of the household followed down to the barn for the unveiling. Michael slid the barn door to the right and walked in.

"This is nice, Michael, but it's not a barn, is it?" Charley asked. "It looks more like an office."

"It used to be a barn. I'm not a farmer and don't plan to farm significantly in the future. CeCe and I both share it as a workspace now. She has the top and uses it more like a studio. I use the bottom as an office space."

Charley looked around at all the details. He was ready to ask more when he heard CeCe call out.

CeCe lifted her arm and waved to everyone to the back corner area. "Come over here, everybody!" Charles and Richard looked over her shoulder to see what Rona saw from her position.

Charley took his hand to cover his mouth as he mouthed unknown words. The secret on the floor was made of six golden puppies romping and frolicking around the floor with their mother eyeing the guests. One look at Michael, and the mother hurriedly got up to meet Michael's hand. Then she sniffed the other visitors and gave two barks, as if she was greeting them.

"This is what you've been hiding out here!" Richard remarked. "Well, how about that? This little fellow looks like the king of the litter," as he spied the most rambunctious puppy of the grouping and stroked his back. "They all look very healthy, too," Richard commented. One darted out from behind the others and ran for Charley's feet.

"Howdy, little guy," Charley said to the blonde wiggly fur ball as he kneeled to tickle the puppy above his ears. The pup moved closer to sniff and lick his hand. After several seconds, the pup pulled itself on top of Charley's boots and started tugging at his paint legs. "What's up, my friend? Do you want to go somewhere, or do you think that hairy leg is a drumstick you'd like to chew on for a while?" Charley said as he put the soft creature back down, where the pup wrestled with another in the litter.

CeCe interrupted the play by touching Charley on the shoulder and saying, "We thought you would like to have one, Charley."

Charley was speechless for a moment as memories returned from another similar gift he had once received. His eyes moistened, but he held back the emotion.

Michael gave Charley a few seconds and then asked, "Would you like to have a puppy? If you can't take it on the plane, we can bring it to you. It would not be a problem. I can bring it."

Still engaged with the puppy, Charley said, "Yes, most definitely yes! I want to have this one. He has a personality. Look at those eyes. He's got energy, and he's playful." Charley intently watched the puppy play with his siblings. "He is bold, but not too aggressive. This pup is a smart little fellow, too. Look at how he pulls his toys out of the crate. He looks at all the possibilities, and then he gets the toy. How did you know, Michael, that I would want this breed?"

"Know what, Charley?" Michael responded with a blank face.

"Did you know I had a puppy like him once?"

"No." Michael's brows raised, questioning the significance.

"It was a long time ago." Charley sat on the floor and let the puppy come running back to him, crawling on his lap and putting his nose under Charley's palm so that he would begin playing with the pup again. "He is perfect in every way."

Rona and Richard each watched and scooped up their favorites. "I don't know how you kept them secret, Michael. I never heard a peep out of them when I was outside," remarked Richard.

"The pups and mother have found a place to be comfortable. I let them out on the other side of the barn when you were busy or not here. It worked out well. I didn't want to tell anyone until Christmas," Michael responded.

"Is Ali taking one?" Rona asked.

"I'm fairly sure she will," Michael responded. "My mother hasn't seen them yet, but she has asked for a puppy in the past."

"I think she'll take that one," Charley said as he pointed to the one that stayed by the smallest pup in the litter. "Ali will sense the protective nature of that little one and won't be able to resist it." The puff of fur looked up at Charley with its doe-like eyes and received the attention those dark eyes seemed to seek. Charley put the little blanket next to the pup and engaged in a bit of play with the ball. With that, the rest of the litter engaged in the playful activity.

Michael reflected on what Charley had said concerning his mother's litter preference as he and CeCe returned to the house. "Interesting observation about my mother," Michael said to CeCe when they were alone. "He is right; Mother is like that. I never thought about that before. Charley remembers a lot more about my mother than I know, and he hasn't seen her in over twenty-five years." Michael wondered what had happened back then to have caused the drift.

CeCe hugged her husband and responded, "Ali and Charley said more in their silence when we were altogether than what they said to each other. Charley had a smile on his face as he listened to the banter between us all. Your mother's eyes sparked the entire night. Your mother can converse with anyone on any subject. But she was spot on last night, as if she was invigorated. I knew they would get along as they both have impeccable manners, but it was magical to see them so respectful and warm to one another, given that it had been so long. There is more than an old flame between them. We'll see what happens next. We said we would not push or manipulate the connection. Let the river go where it wants to flow."

"Absolutely," Michael responded as he tossed a chocolate candy CeCe's way.

The afternoon provided some quiet time. Charley

had taken the time to put on some warm clothes and take a run. Michael asked to join, and they found an opportunity to be together alone. "I'm not a fast runner, but I can do 3-5 miles depending on the terrain and weather," Charley commented. "How did you find this place?"

"It was my mother's grandparent's home, and she inherited it from them. She grew up here, and we lived here as I was growing up. Mother bought the inn about five years ago, and it had an apartment for the owner added to the back of the inn, but she never really used it as her own. When CeCe and I got married, mother gave us this house, this place to live. She moved to the inn and remodeled it, using the furnishings of her choice. Did she take you on tour last night?"

"No, we mostly stayed in her office on the first floor or outside. However, what I saw was very impressive." Charley commented.

"My mother has a genuine talent for decorating. She has great taste in everything," Michael said. "I have changed the house and barn to make it fit CeCe's and my needs. I would have probably bought some cookie-cutter home in a larger town if Mother had not allowed us to live on this property, but it suits us now. I did not think CeCe would like it initially, but I think it has grown on her, and she travels a bit. CeCe and my mother have been talking about working together by owning an old-time bakery down from the inn. She loved some ideas she saw in Savannah while we were there. It might work fine. Mother loves to create food as much as she loves to write. I don't know. She can get stressed sometimes when she has too many plates spinning. I don't criticize her for that, though, as she is incredibly talented, and I don't have half her skills and energy."

Charley slowed down to turn his pace into a walk. He gazed out over the rolling hills. "What was it like Michael to growing up?"

Michael took a few seconds before responding. "I was like any other kid. I pushed some limits. But I would not hurt my mom or my grandparents while they were still living. I was an excellent student, which helped me stay out of trouble because it allowed me more opportunities. I always had an inner voice that pushed me to learn, give the best I could, and become somebody. When I could have drifted away, that kept me out of danger."

"You must have missed not having a father," Charley commented.

Michael tried to be as honest as he could with what he knew of himself. "In some ways, you don't miss something you never had. However, as I've gotten more years behind me, I see things surface within in me I know are a part of not having the experience. I try to deal with faith issues. Others use alcohol or some other means to soothe the beast. You are a pastor, Charley. I suspect you know what I mean."

Charley responded. "Yes, perhaps. We all have deep needs that only God knows how to meet." Charley stopped for a moment to look at Michael directly. "I want you to know that you were created for this world by two people who loved you. Your mother and I took different paths, so I am sorry. You missed having a physical father around you when you were growing up. I believe the heavenly father brought you to my church that day, and grace touched my heart. Only God would understand what would wake me up and allow me to see another facet of Him. I am humbled. He used me to create the wonderful man that you have become. I cannot think any higher of your mother for raising you than she did."

"Maybe things turned out the way they were supposed to be," Michael said as he touched Charley's shoulder gently. "We face things about ourselves, which are part of growing up."

The evening finally fell, with the fireplace blazing and a pot of gumbo on the stove. Ali made the trip with her vehicle filled with gifts, food, and an old guitar case. Rona and Richard were delighted to have one last night with everyone.

"Charley, why don't you tell us something you would like to do when you're not preaching? Most ministers I know like to read and are studious. What about you?"

"I'm more of a service personality, but I like to be

creative too. I have something coming up on freight tomorrow for CeCe and Michael. I do not want to say too much, except I made it. That's what I do in my spare time. I make things. That leads to meeting people, and the next thing you know, there's something essential to talk about."

"What do you make?" asked Richard.

"I like to work with textures. I enjoy using my hands to create. Usually, I am at my happiest when I am working with wood. After that, I dabble in making furniture or doing millwork. Sometimes, I go in another direction if I'm given the opportunity to do something or work with someone else with skills I don't have. For me, it feels like composing a piece of music. It is my personal church experience." Charley then looked at Ali and continued. "Ali was always like that too, except she used words, and sometimes she would dabble in painting." He turned to Ali and smiled at her. "Do you still like to paint, Ali?" Charley asked. "Your watercolor paints were my favorite."

"I still do a little. I only paint when I am in the mood. It's not as easy as writing, where I sit down and put ideas down on paper. It is a guilty pleasure. It takes a little more time and effort to pull out the paint, brushes, and everything that goes with it. I do not think I have the gift for it, although I could probably technically complete a piece if I pushed myself. I need that flame stirring in me to get me doing anything. My time is so limited that I prioritize. But, like today, I felt the need to make some of these." Ali walked over to Michael and handed him a tin.

Charley teased Ali. "Wait a minute. Yesterday you told me you hadn't had pizza in seven years, but now you're saying cookies are all right?"

"Charley, if you must know, I eat plenty of other stuff besides pizza! Cookies are one of those rare treats I enjoy along with my tree bark tea and spinach leaves, right, Richard?"

"That's what Rona keeps telling me, anyway." Richard moved over to his wife and gave her a whiff of the chocolate-drenched oatmeal and walnut delicacy. "Rona, can we have more of this with my cup of green tea every day? I might be just a little less cranky when I'm at home." Richard took a whiff himself before he took his first bite of pleasure.

"Richard, you can eat whatever you please. My only stipulation is that if you want it, you prepare it and clean it up afterward. Otherwise, you need to eat what I have lovingly prepared to help you stay healthy. That's our deal."

"You are hard to bargain with, but I will stick to our deal. It has some nice perks," Richard joked.

"Richard, we've been married for over thirty years now, and you appear in fine shape, so I believe I have taken excellent care of you," Rona chimed back.

"You have, honey bun! I'm not complaining in the

least." Richard teased. The room filled with soft laughter. The comical swordplay between Richard and his wife was characteristic of their relationship. CeCe recalled what it was like growing up in their house as a child. She knew her mother and father were equal partners in a successful relationship. Arguments came and went, but the glue that kept the family together never failed. The bond was an undefined commitment that was never verbally spoken, but always put in each action consistently daily. CeCe knew it was a gift and wanted to nurture it in her marriage to Michael. As Michael looked her way, laughing at her father's humor, she felt Michael wanted the same relationship deep within.

Charley snapped up a cookie and took a generous bite. "Wow, these are good! Do you serve these at the inn, Ali?"

Ali enjoyed the compliments, as this had been this week's experiment in the kitchen. "I haven't served this cookie yet. However, I have freshly baked cookies often. I love to try new things. The staff helps too. CeCe and I have been testing out some recipes to see if we could find a successful assortment of items that might be popular with people. We have shared the idea of creating a little bakery in the town. This recipe is from an old cookbook I came across in a shop in Winston-Salem. I tinkered with the recipe. I like the creativity with cooking." She looked at Charley for a moment. "I have found there's a lot of me I enjoy."

"I can honestly say we are the benefactors of your

creativity," Michael responded as he finished the last bite.

Some hours later, Charley sat in the overstuffed chair in the den. He watched the flames flicker along with the colors splintering from the fire. The moment hadn't come yet, but the pastor from Savannah was a patient man. His time was almost up, and he would return to Savannah tomorrow. Would there be a right time? Charley looked away for a moment as he reached for a mug of coffee on the side table. He glimpsed the night sky through the gap in the drapes and pondered over the chance to see a brilliant star making its presence. Finally, Charley settled back in his chair and closed his eyes. His spiritual eyes saw a young man sitting around another fire's glow, thinking the same thoughts. Would fate be cruel and write the same ending? Charley finally put his mind to rest before walking back to his room. Your way, God, that's all there is for me.

Across the fields a few miles away, a small light could be seen seeping through the interior shutters of a room in the back of the inn where an apartment existed for its owner. Ali sat, turning pages from an old book that looked heavily worn. She rubbed her neck and Ali got up to turn off the light on the table next to the window. Once the room darkened, she moved the shutter lever to look at the sky in the twilight hours. God had a heart for women seeking his love, Ali believed. Some women never get past searching for that love in earthly relationships. Ali had learned that the disappointments in relationships could bring one closer to faith in God, leaving those needs in his hands. She was content all these years by raising Michael and using her gifts of hospitality and storytelling to serve others creatively. Ali was contemplating the meaning of all that had happened since Charley's arrival. She was happy to see him again, but where was this leading?

Early the following day, the house was full of activity. Smells from the kitchen of coffee and bacon permeated the path from the stairs to the kitchen. Michael had come in from the outside, washing his hands and rubbing them, bringing warmth to his fingers. "It's a chilly morning, but the roads look clear, and they have dried off. I will be careful to avoid ice patches. It should be a pleasant ride to the airport. We can go after breakfast."

"I have something for you. Let me go get it," said Charley.

"Okay. We have your pup here. If you can wait till February, I will bring your dog down to you. That is only six weeks away. We will make sure no one else claims it, including Mother, who had her eye on the one you picked." Michael smiled with a mischievous grin at CeCe.

Charley walked to the hall and pulled something out of the outside pouch of his carry-on. He returned. He said,

"Your mother can fight me for it, but I'd give in; don't tell her that. I wanted to give you something, but I changed my mind last night. Would you mind giving your mother this package? It is something I have held on to for a long time. Your mother will know what to do with it.

Michael took the package from Charley and took it to another room. "I'll make sure she gets it."

"By the way, did she buy you the dog that had puppies?" Charley asked.

"No. CeCe and I agreed on Shelby together. Why do you ask?"

"It's nothing. It's just that your mother bought me a pup just like that once when we were dating. It was a long time ago," Charley answered.

The ride to the airport was a quiet one for both men. Michael walked with Charley as far as he could go without a ticket.

"I would have loved you as soon as you came into this world, Michael," Charley whispered in Michael's ear as he hugged him goodbye. He quickly turned and moved towards the security check at the terminal. Charley turned back to make one last look and waved goodbye. He knew if he lingered longer, his emotions would flow out in an uncontrolled rush of tears. But he had faith enough to trust.

Chapter 4

TWO MONTHS LATER PASSED since Charley left Michael's home for Christmas. It was February and a favorite time of the year for Charley back in Savannah. He felt refueled by the recent growth emerging on the scene each day, so he came to the church office early, thinking he would be more disciplined working in the office than at home.

"Charley, would you like me to order lunch for your today, or would you like to go out for a while?" He heard a voice talking to him from the doorway.

"I'm good, but thank you," he called out. Charley knew his thoughts were fluttering around the office like moths. He had checked his watch frequently in the last two hours, thinking that more time had passed. Michael planned to come to Savannah that weekend. He wanted to stay available in the downtown area should Michael call and ask to meet somewhere. Michael called around noon but said he would not be stopping by today. When Charley casually asked about Beaux, Michael assured Charley that the pup was being cared for and made the trip fine, as planned. Beaux would be delivered to him later that day. He has more information later in the day. Charley thought that was odd but figured that maybe an employee for the company may have taken a fancy to the pup and volunteered to watch over him while Michael was busy.

Charley replied to Michael, "I am planning to leave the office around two today, so if you want me to pick up Beaux somewhere, let me know. I have everything all set for him at home. I have the studio ready also, so if you want to stay over this weekend, there is a key for you under the frog by the door." Charley admitted he was disappointed not to see Michael that day, but some things are selfish desires.

"Thanks. I will talk again with you on Saturday," Michael responded. The conversation ended, and Charley was left to his thoughts. He continued working on his correspondence and passed on an offer to lunch with some staff. Fridays usually were short days for everyone, so Charley appreciated the time alone to finish reviewing some documents that had not been scanned and emailed but still needed his attention. As the time dragged into the afternoon hours, he glanced at the time on his computer. Charley stretched his back and stood up, looking outside through the window. The traffic was creeping through the square, typical for a Friday afternoon. Charley contemplated his next move and elected to finish for the day. In anticipation of Michael being in town, Charley's mind was sifting through a list of the errands he wanted to do on the way home. He had aired out the studio above the garage just in case Michael preferred to stay there, even though there was a spare room in the main house. Just as Charley was locking up, a young man who went to church intermittently and attended one of the local colleges walked down the street. They conversed for a few minutes. An idea came to Charley, and he offered the student some handyperson chores at the church during spring break, which the young man gladly accepted. It was a winning situation for both sides. Charley needed hands to help with some of his projects. The students were always in need of a little extra money. Plus, it allowed the students to make friends and network with others they may not have typically met. Charley left the young man and took a few steps closer to the sidewalk, taking him to private parking.

"I wondered when your boss was going to let you go today!" a female voice said as Charley entered the parking area. The driver's side window of a gray RV was rolled down and made a woman sit inside. Charley instantly stopped in his path. The plates said Pennsylvania, but the dialect was closer to a mixture of cosmopolitan and elegance. The voice had a familiar quality. That voice had flowed in and out of his thoughts each night since Christmas Eve.

"Ma'am, do you know this is private parking?" Charley grinned as he took a few steps closer to the vehicle's open window.

"Oh, I do. The police officer asked me that five minutes ago. I told him I was waiting for an important person at church today."

"And he believed you?" Charley's grin grew into a smile with a twinkle in his eyes.

"Oh yes, I told him that Reverend Charles Howard had a visitor he held in the highest regard. The officer was pleasant and allowed me to stay as I was here for the pastor. I did not tell a lie, did I?" Ali looked up with eyes as wide as a doe's. "You will cover for me, won't you, if he comes back again and asks me more questions?"

Charley laughed from his belly as he looked closer at the passengers inside. "I think the Reverend will vouch that this is a significant guest." He reached in, pushed the release button to open the door, and gingerly picked up the creamed, color-furred pup from the driver's lap. He took the leash that Ali had already put on the puppy, gently cradled him, and lowered him to the pavement, all while Beaux wiggled and licked Charley's neck. "We need to let Beaux stretch his legs some," Charley said with tenderness.

"Yes," Ali spoke to Charley, looking directly into his eyes. She said nothing else but awaited Charley's response.

He paused for a moment, reading her face. One glance into her searching eyes let him know she was not talking about Beaux. "Good," Charley responded, not giving his thoughts away. "So, you are the delivery method that Michael was talking about earlier when I asked about Beaux. He certainly did not let on at all that it would be you. Ali Taylor, you certainly are a special surprise today!"

She raised her chin and said, "Yes, I will." Ali looked up and searched his face again for a hint that he understood her message. His face was blank. She then turned away slightly to mask her disappointment. She boldly looked back again, this time with a tighter lip and a defensiveness in her eyes.

Charley's facial expression softened. "I heard you, Ali." Charley took a deep breath and showed a warmer, broader smile back. "Is that your answer?"

"Yes, it is," Ali responded with confusion as she guessed Charley's next move. She thought she saw a flash of light in Charley's eyes. Or was it the sun? Finally, she swung her legs out and stood straight before him.

"I guess you opened the package," Charley said seriously.

"The one with the story I wrote for you to read over Christmas break when we were in college?" Ali asked with a smile.

Charley felt like he was dancing the tango with a very skilled partner. Ali was just that kind of woman, especially with words. "Yes, that package."

"There was something else in that package, too. Was it true, all of it?" Ali asked.

"Yes, it was," Charley said stoically. He knew what Ali was alluding to with her question. But he did not want to expose the nature of his thoughts as they ran deep into his soul. "Can we go for a walk?" Charley asked.

"Yes," Ali responded. *However, had she misunderstood the significance of Charley's act of leaving her the envelope at Christmas?* Its contents held souvenirs of a Christmas holiday they had shared in Savannah almost thirty years before.

Charley smiled and responded, "Let me welcome you to my city, Ali. Savannah and all its beauty can't hold a candle to the one I am looking at now. Did you bring what I left for you?"

Ali nodded affirmatively. As he remained silent, Ali responded. "Well then, let's see if Beaux likes his new home." Ali could not connect with Charley's thoughts or feelings. However, as they began their stroll down the street, she could imagine the face of a young man she used to know behind the darkened shades and the salt and pepper waves of his hair. He is still there, Ali reassured herself. If anything, he was now more of the person she always thought him to be mature, wise, and elegant, yet masculine. She thought of the missing piece broken off and set adrift many years ago. Could the lost half be finally found?

Charley looked down at the soft rhinestone collar and quipped. "She's dressed you all fancy, Beaux, and probably spoiled you, too. I bet she hasn't taken you to the beach to play frisbee! You are going to love that!" Charley said to his furry companion as he scrunched down and scratched his fuzzy ears. "I will win you back!" Charley teasingly spoke to Beaux, but intended for Ali's ears. Charley tugged on the leash and gently guided the pup down the street. He reached over to Ali, coaxed her hand with his, and led the way onto the uneven sidewalk, uplifted by old tree roots and settling cement that came about with age.

"You know, I met Michael and CeCe at a place just down that avenue as he pointed to a busy café with people clustered around outdoor tables. It's a favorite spot for locals downtown during the day. Out-of-towners usually find it by accident as it is away from the river and the hotels. That Sunday, I was drawn to go there by myself. I walked a couple of blocks and stopped in, never thinking I was walking to meet someone that would open my heart, lungs, liver, and brain again," Charley said with a laugh. "Let's cross the street, and I'll show you something else." Charley walked a few blocks west of the church, where a small building stood. It appeared cared for, with planted shrubbery and a fresh coat of paint. Charley picked up Beaux in his arms and opened the door for Ali. A small reception area stood beside a larger door, and children's voices carried from beyond the wall.

"Sounds like we have some little people today in there," Charley said to the young lady at the desk.

"Reverend Howard, it is Friday, and that means the Mother's Day Out program is going on inside," the young lady said with excitement when she saw who the individual was talking to her in the reception area. "Today's activity was a dance troupe who came in and taught the kids some dance moves. I think they are taking a break now. And who is that you brought today?" She moved around the desk to give Beaux a pat on his head and smiled up at Ali. "He is a precious puppy. The children are going to love him!"

"Yes, I think Beaux will make lots of friends today. We are going to take a walk around. Kelly. Ms. Taylor is part of why we have this beautiful building, and I want her to see what she means to us here."

"I am pleased to meet you, Ms. Taylor, and thank you for allowing us to remodel the old bank and let us bring something back to the city!" Kelly said with enthusiasm.

Ali smiled graciously but a little hesitantly as she looked at Charley. "Please show me more, Reverend Howard." She followed his lead down a small corridor and through another door. Ali pulled on Charley's arm and asked, "What did she mean by that?"

"Let's look inside," Charley responded without answering Ali's question directly. Behind the doors was an open space, and children sat around tables with colored mats stacked around the side for a tumbling class. "This activity center is what you helped us create."

"Reverend Howard!" a young man came from off the stage. "You just missed seeing our dance troupe perform today."

"Thank you for coming and being here for the kids today!" replied Reverend Howard. "Thank you so much. I bet everyone had a great time!" Charley looked around and saw two youthful faces eyeing each other and getting closer to the Reverend and Ali as they talked to the troupe leader.

"Can we pet your puppy, Reverend Howard?" a youngster called out. The petite little girl with ribbons reached out to touch the soft fur of Beaux's floppy ears.

"Yes, be gentle, as he is just getting to know everyone and is probably a little scared. We want to show him how much we like him without frightening him," Charley said to the children. More of the youngsters came up and circled Beaux. Charley wove around each child to allow each to have the chance to touch the wiggling bundle of fur. "I think Beaux must like you as he lets you get close. Not all dogs are friendly, so we should always ask the owner if it's safe to pet them. I think Beaux will want to come back and see you all, too. I might need to arrive earlier next time so you can teach me some dance moves."

One of the little boys named Jamal did a simple twist of the arms and shuffled his feet. "Charley honored the young boy's talent and had him hold Beaux as he tried to imitate the same move. Everyone laughed. Charley said his goodbyes to Jordan and the children and took Beaux back. He led Ali past the gathering and through another door on the other side of the room.

"Do you spend a lot of time here, Charley?" Ali asked.

"Not that much time. There are a lot of places I need to be. We use this space for a lot of different functions. There are a lot of different needs in the community. We can't meet all the needs, but there are some needs we can address. Giving mother's a free afternoon off while allowing children to make friends and have fun in a safe environment is something the church and some sponsors can do. We have lots of people here giving their time. A few are paid employees. The church bought the building in a somewhat needy state. We received a large donation from an unexpected benefactor who seeded the project. Other small amounts came in when the work began." Charley stopped for a moment and looked directly at Ali. "Michael provided that initial amount. I assumed that you somehow in-fluenced him."

"Charley, I didn't. I swear I did not! Another source

must have influenced Michael. I may have always said kind words about you as he was growing up, but I did not encourage him to be generous because you were his father. I didn't provide the funds. That came from Michael's heart or another source." She paused in silence for a moment and spoke out of kindness to Charley. "I believe a child can feel a parent's love even when that parent is unknown to him. I am thrilled that you showed me this and that Michael supported this project. I want to take credit, but that belongs to someone else."

Charley accepted Ali's answer as the truth. However, with Ali's denial, it was still a mystery where and how the funds came to be. Charley and Ali began walking up the street. Stopping for iced tea at the local coffeehouse was a quick diversion. From there, they eventually walked back to their parked vehicles. "Let's go home, Ali." He pulled out a pen and a piece of paper from his pocket. "Here's the address and directions in case you lose me in the traffic."

"I will take Beaux with me as he feels comfortable riding," Ali responded.

"Beaux, do you hear that?" Charley rubbed the puppy's head. "She wants you back. She will have a hard time letting you go, my friend." Charley looked up at Ali and shrugged his shoulders. "You win round won, but let's see what Beaux thinks when he sees his new bachelor's pad," Charley said with a grin that warmed Ali's heart. "It should be easy to keep you in sight driving this," Charley said as he touched the van's cab. "You still have that gypsy spirit!" Charley laughed. "I have missed that, Ali. Follow me home."

Charley's residence was near the marsh on one of the barrier islands. His parents had left him a home in the city limits of Savannah, but he sold that a few years after they passed away, to everyone's surprise. Instead, he moved closer to the water. The home was small and had a cottage vibe, and the home's bones had a comfortable feel. The previous owners had done fine landscaping that suited Charley's taste. He spent most of his time remodeling a small studio apartment above the garage when he bought the place. Charley had designed an enlarged cupola-like structure from the upper loft, something he spotted in pictures from magazines of homes dotting Maine's sea cliffs. The studio acted as an office, guest room, and favorite place to relax, with a décor that reflected his interests in woodworking and design talents and, of course, the beauty of the sea. Not everyone knew of Charley's gift. However, many had seen his work without knowing the creator. The main cottage home was just a few feet away, simple in architecture, with a fresh coat of golden yellow paint and white trim. It gave a clean, welcoming appearance from the street.

Ali enjoyed the drive over the last two days. The change of scenery from the rolling hills of Pennsylvania to the lowlands of the coastal region was quite distinct. Water ruled the coastal lands, shaping the inter-coastal waterways, wetlands, and shorelines. Only the creator could truly understand and control the power of the water. Unfortunately, humanity just thought they could. Ali followed Charley into the drive and parked her vehicle on the extra parking pad. She looked around and processed all that she was feeling. Thirty years had passed since the relationship had started. Did it end when she left that day? There was a dream-like quality as she looked at her surroundings. Ali tried to squelch her racing thoughts. Could this be our time?

Charley came to open the door. "This is home, Ali. It's eclectic, but I've enjoyed the surroundings since I moved away from the major thoroughfare where my parents lived. It's a smaller place, but it has character. Or maybe it's a character that owns the place!" Charley joked with gentleness in his eyes and a smile on his lips.

Ali looked around and smiled back directly at Charley. "I see a lot of character all around me, and most of all, I see the Charles I knew. It's beautiful!"

"I'm glad. That makes me feel hopeful. I liked it me too, most of the time. I have more callouses on my hands and, hopefully, wiser now." Charley walked a few more paces across the sandy soil mixed with tufts of grass. "I had things ready for Michael, but I think it will be your liking, too. Come this way, Ali. I built this studio over the garage. It will give you your own private space for now. I will take anything upstairs. You feel you need to freshen up, and then I can help you later unload what you want to bring inside." Charley took the leash from Ali and looked down at the pup, sniffing his shoes and rubbing against his pant legs. "And Beaux, I have a place just for you too!"

Ali followed, with a few questions in her mind but happy to be escorted to a place she could relax with no one around to watch how she allowed herself to let her guard down and be herself in a situation she was unsure how it would play out. She followed Charley up the stairs and into a bright single room on the garage's second floor with a loft above that. She felt the anxiousness lifting. There was a subtle hint of something in the air, like eucalyptus. A few paintings were on the walls, adding color to white-painted walls and wood floors. The table looked like it had been hand-stained but of the highest quality. A leather recliner sat in one corner. A guitar on a stand was on the right, no television was noted because of Charley's dislike for it. There was a small kitchenette on the back wall with a sink. A couple of overhead cabinets with glass-paneled fronts had been painted white and then finished in a distressed style which matched the finish on the white-painted flooring. A small additional set of stairs went to a well-lit loft area. A table for drafting sat in front of a large window with shutters. "You didn't tell me you owned anything like this when you were in Pennsylvania."

"What's there to say? It's what I've done in my free

time. There wasn't anything here except an unfinished two-story garage opened to the raptors when I bought this place. A wasp nest and a small attic window with broken glass allowed the bats to come in freely. I remember that detail. Also, it's been therapeutic for me to work here, away from the downtown area. I can take off my shirt and get sweaty, and no one is around to gawk."

"Charley, it's fabulous!" Ali whispered, with tears welling up in her eyes. "It's just like…" and Ali stopped to rephrase her thoughts. "It's what I see in magazines or books on design."

Charley chuckled with a light in his brown eyes. "Wow, do you think I'm that good?" He came closer to kiss her on the cheek. "Thank you, Ali. I appreciate those words and hold them right here," as he pressed her hand to his heart. "There is not much to take you around and see in the studio. There is a loft up there where you can sleep. There is a simple shower behind this door." Charley opened the door to show a shower built into a closet space. "If you want a hot bath, you can come to the main house. It has a little kitchenette area here to make some coffee, keep some drinks cold, or have some food while one is hanging out up here. The coffee mugs are up here. I put some snacks and beverages in the refrigerator. There are many popcorn packets in this cabinet, one of Michael's favorite things to do when visiting. Let's walk up to the loft." As they did so, Charley pointed out the cupola structure from the inside, sharing that one could climb and sit above the loft to enjoy the view. "This is everyone's favorite place to come and relax. I got the idea from a cupola design and added a look from a beach house I saw in person once. I then took it to an architect friend to make it fit the project. Sometimes I call it the dome because it's a bigger space than a traditional cupola, but I don't have a word for the area that does it justice."

Ali could envision the sweet picture of Michael climbing up there and eating popcorn, just as Charley described. She wished that she and Charley had experienced all those missing years with those same moments of intimacy. Ali moved closer to Charley and touched his arm. "Charley, we don't have to be separated right now."

"Yes. We do, Ali. We are going to do this right this time. We were young long ago, and maybe we made some mistakes. But we might have a second chance. I will not make a mistake with the most precious thing I thought I had lost forever. I also want you to understand who I am. I'm not a perfect man, but I am a man who believes in and attempts to walk the right path. I'm not talking about just being a pastor. I may not always get it right, but I am walking on a path. I am not asking anyone to walk it with me unless it is right for them to walk from one marker to another. I want you to be sure. I cannot change into someone you think I should be. I may not be my mother's vision of a son or my father's ideal legacy." Charley moved a piece of a fallen bang on Ali's forehead so he could take in the expression from her eyes. "I'm going to let you rest up and get acclimated to this space and surroundings. Then, I will change and put something on the grill at about five-thirty. I will warn you I have some neighbors who seem to gravitate over when I'm on the patio with food, so be prepared for a less-than-quiet night." Charley laughed with warmth in his eyes.

"Beaux, you are coming with me. If you remain in this woman's care much longer, I won't be able to save you from the consequences of being a pampered pooch. The opportunity to have you as my companion and me as your master will be lost." Charley looked at Ali and laughed while shaking his head. "All right, I am out of here. Come down whenever you're ready."

Ali was left alone in this serene setting to face her thoughts and rest for the evening. Charley was shedding layers of himself before her eyes, and she liked what she saw. Ali touched the table and could envision sanding the surface and making each stroke of the stain he must have applied. She walked up the tiny stairs to the loft. Ali opened the window to feel the cool breeze and bathed in the sunlight, allowing her thoughts to flow. The sea breezes filled the room, and she felt refreshed. I am thankful for this day. The morning may bring a storm or another day of clear skies, but it will be a new day. Ali had mentally thrown past mistakes into the water below when she crossed the bridge today. Let her mistakes float away where no one else would know or count them. She could not control if others would judge her in self-righteousness, but she had the power to believe in how God saw her in his eyes. She was not responsible for their thoughts, only her own. Ali climbed above the sleeping area to the space at the top of the room. Immediately, she was surrounded by more light, delighting her with joy. The shimmering rays danced in her eyes from the reflected light of the high tides rolling in to fill the marshes that adjoined the bluffs a few blocks away. She marked a new day in her life today. She started a new life filled with unknowns and some old dreams.

A little into the early evening, Charley went to the backyard to start the grill. He smiled when he heard the door from the studio open and close. "Well, you look rested," said a voice from behind the lid of a gas grill. "I have some water and sodas in the ice chest over there. And, in the refrigerator, there is some sweet tea. If you like it with lemon, there is one in the bottom drawer. I usually keep my tea simple, but others may like it with a bit more punch. Is there anything that you need?" Charley asked.

Ali walked over to where Charley was busy at work, gazing around the backyard and then soaking in the image of Charley being present in his environment. "This is nice, Charley," Ali said, feeling cheerful. She walked to the ice chest and looked inside before pulling out a bottle of sparkling water. "You have a lot of cans and bottles here. Are you expecting a lot of guests?"

"Guests?" Charley laughed. "They're not real

guests as you might define the word, but I expect the smell and sight of burgers on the grill will draw a few folks through the hedge within the next fifteen minutes. They are a kind of family without bloodlines. I saw my neighbor pull in about thirty minutes ago. He's already shouted over the shrubbery that he and his family were coming over for dinner. Be prepared!" Charley had a slight grin, but he didn't reveal anything else.

"That's nice to have neighbors you get along with so well. I am eager to meet them," Ali responded as she looked around for something she could do.

Charley's smile got a little bigger, but he kept on with his duties and did not look at Ali directly. "You are so skilled at menu planning and decorating the table. I'm a little embarrassed here in your presence. Why don't you raid my refrigerator and cabinets and see what you can do to make a salad? I have some big bowls in the pantry, and there might be something else you can find on the shelves. I am going to let you fend for yourself in there. The kitchen is beyond that door. I hear voices from the yard next door, so let me start some hamburgers," Charley said.

Bob noted the extra vehicle in Charley's drive when he pulled in from work. Charley must be having some visitors this evening. He wasn't sure if dinner at 6:00 at Charley's was on the calendar. Still, when Charley called out to invite the family over, Bob was eager to accept. Thirty minutes later, Bob yelled over the hedge. "Hope you got some room on that grill because I'm coming over with a stash of my own," said a man, pushing his way through the foliage. He strolled over to where Charley was standing, carrying a sealed container of bratwurst in his left hand and a package of buns in his right. "Here, get these started on the heat," Charley's neighbor said as he got closer.

"Will do. There's room," Charley replied.

Bob turned toward sounds he heard coming from Charley's kitchen. Bob waved blindly at the outline of a person he could see from the window. He looked back at Charley. "You are sure it's fine? We don't want to interfere."

"No, Ali knows my neighbors are coming for dinner. I want her to meet you and your family. You might say it would be nice to welcome her here as part of the extended family." The corners of Charley's mouth slightly drew upward without giving his true feelings or thoughts away to his neighbor.

"Sure!" Bob responded. He looked back at Charley quizzically. "Anything I need to know?" But before Charley could answer, Ali came out of the kitchen. Her arms filled with paper plates and napkins kept her from waving to the stranger. Bob made no delays by greeting Ali. "Hi! I'm Bob from next door."

"It's nice to meet you, Bob. I'm Ali. From what Charley tells me, I'm the newcomer to this party. I hope you will tell me about all the wild stories you have about your neighbor here," Ali said as she walked closer to

Charley. "You must have a few."

"You can't pry a single story from these lips," Bob joked with a toothy, white smile. "Charley has too much stuff on me!"

"He is so right!" Charley said as he shook his head and continued to flip the burgers. He looked up for a moment at the group and then went on cooking the meat, laughing to himself, knowing the secret.

Ali laughed and gave Bob a wink. "We'll have to pull some of those confessions from him. It's been thirty years since I last saw him, and I know there's a trunk full of crazy, wild abandonment antics that he is hiding behind his calm demeanor."

Bob responded, "Well, since you got Charley pegged, I'm not sure I can add much, but I might verify a few stories if he lets a few out tonight!"

"Oh, no. I'm not telling my side of the story until you share your side first," Charley joked.

"There you go, Ali. We swore to protect our tales of past crazy behavior," Bob said with a grin. "However, if you should pry a tale or two from me after a few drinks, I will deny everything I said!"

Ali laughed. "Well, I go back to the kitchen and snooped through a few cabinets and drawers. Give me a few minutes, and I will return with some edible creation."

After Ali went back inside, Bob probed Charley for

answers to questions he had. "Charley, I'm sensing something here. Is Ali someone I know? Is there something I don't know going on here?"

Charley shrugged his shoulder. "You know Ali, Frogman."

"Wait a minute!" Bob exclaimed. "You haven't said that since college. Let me put this together. Ali is her name. I know her. The auto plates are from out of state." Bob kept thinking. "Ali! It's our study buddy, Ali! That's who is in the kitchen?" Bob asked incredulously.

Charley nodded his head affirmatively. "She brought me my new pup, Beaux. That traitor is probably basking at her feet right now, getting all the attention. I need to separate those two, or I will never get them apart!" Charley said with a sarcastic tone and amusement on his face.

"That is Ali, and she is here in your house with your dog raiding your kitchen?" Bob asked in astonishment. Bob recovered from the surprise and gave a broad smile.

"Let me go in and get some more ice for this tub. I will be right back!" Bob left the backyard to pursue his curiosity and his excitement.

Charley's neighbor caught Ali pouring the dressing on the salad when he entered the kitchen. She looked in his direction and sent a warm smile to him as he drew closer. Bob stopped in his tracks and gazed in astonishment with his mouth half-opened. Words flowed from his mouth, but his brain was still in shock as he quickly filtered files in his memory. "Ali, it is you!"

Ali looked a little more intent at the man she was staring at in the kitchen, questioning who this stranger could be.

"Ali, it's Frogman!" Bob said with excitement.

The name pricked Ali's attention. She stared at him and thought. Her eyes began to shine and grow larger than her smile grew more prominent. "Bob, you are Frogman?" Ali questioned in disbelief. "How did you find your way here?" She walked over to give Bob a friendly hug.

"Well, just a few feet across the myrtles, I turned east to come through the back door!" Bob responded with humor. "I have changed in appearance, like no hair and a few wrinkles around the eyes. Charley and I are neighbors! I helped him buy this place."

Ali's cheeks glowed. "I would have never recognized you. I can't believe I am seeing you after all these years. Wow! Seeing you here in Charley's house is a wild but pleasant surprise! You were not from Savannah, were you?"

"No, I moved here several years ago to instruct and do research for the university. It was closer to my wife's parents, so we moved rather than living in a larger city where the pace makes one old, quickly. When I was in the area, I always looked Charley up. He and I always kept in touch. We've been the best of friends for most of our adult life. Carole and I took notice of the house next door when we moved. Charley always liked the property, but it wasn't like it is now. The owner told me he wanted to sell the home one day. I let Charley know. He bought the property from the owner, and we have been neighbors ever since. That's my story. So, you and Charley, have you kept in touch?" Bob asked.

"No, not for the last thirty years. I will let Charley tell his story as it's probably more interesting," Ali said, avoiding further questions she wasn't ready to talk about with others.

"It is great to have you here! Charley has done a lot with this place. He needs to show you everything. So, what about you?" Bob asked.

"I live in Pennsylvania and own an inn in one of those quaint, small towns. I am also a writer. Those two things alone keep me a recluse for most of the year. However, I travel every chance I get. I must do a bit more planning now so that everything is covered. I'm still dazed from being here, so I don't have much to say. I'll talk about myself later. I'm just enjoying every moment right now."

"I'm profoundly stunned, in a good way, to see you again. I am dying to hear about how you and Charley met again. I cannot wait until we all sit for dinner to-night and hear that story. Now, I will get some more ice out of this freezer and be on my way outdoors so we can get this party started." He glanced over at the kitchen counter where Ali was working. "What is that I see walnuts, avocados, spinach, and feta cheese? Did this come from Charley's kitchen? Besides hamburgers and hot dogs, I have hardly seen him keep anything gourmet beyond organic peanut butter. If I knew he had that stash in his kitchen, I would come over and raid it more often. Maybe that's why he hides the good stuff when I'm around!" Bob laughed and sent her a wink before stealing a walnut from the bowl. "Oh well, let me get on with my duties here. Do you need any help with carrying anything outside?"

"No, I'm fine. I'm just going to toss a few things together and follow right behind you," responded Ali. "It's good to see you again, and I know we'll get to talk more later on."

Bob grabbed a metal object looking like a small washtub from behind the closet door and dumped the bag of ice inside. He reached for the doorknob and heartily responded to Ali. "I want to introduce you to my wife and kids when you come outside. That means Carole and my daughter with her fiancé, David, who I am being forced under protest to adopt as my bigger and smarter future son-in-law. Of course, nobody's too good for my princess, but if I have to like the boys she brings home, this would be the best of the lot." He halted for a moment and looked back around. Bob's face showed kindness when he had an afterthought.

"Ali, Charley is a good guy. You can trust him to do right and be a good man." With that, Bob walked outside, leaving Ali to her thoughts.

Ali watched through the window. A little tear escaped her eye as she felt something deep inside change. She twitched her nose to hold back the sniffle. Is this what it is like to feel accepted? She had shut a small part of her heart away so many years ago, and with just a few words, a sliver of light touched some place deep inside. A glass pane in a window in her heart had been washed clean. A speck of dirty, painful words sent to her by another had just disappeared. "Thank you, Frogman. It's been a long time since I've seen you, my old friend." Ali whispered for know one else to hear.

"Charley, you've been hiding a secret," Bob said as he dropped the tub and bag of ice on a side table. Charley's muscles tensed throughout his body. "You have more in your cabinets than peanut butter. Dinner is going to be good, really, really, really fantastic!"

Charley shook his head and replied. "Here, take over." Charley gave up the spatula to Bob and wiped his hands. "Welcome, Carole. Come on over and set that right over there. So, what did you bring?"

Carole was a petite blonde who looked like she had spent her days between the tennis court and the salon. Her personality was bubbling wherever she was except while attending a lecture on the latest physical properties on some uninteresting topic. Bob had learned to share a ride with another colleague on one of those evenings. However, sharing Carole's company on a fishing boat or water ski or even at the old-fashioned carwash could be the best day of one's life, Bob often mused to himself.

Before Carole could answer, Bob broke in. "Charley has a guest tonight, Carole. You will love meeting her!"

Carole took the bait and smiled broadly without comment. "Just something quick tonight," Carole responded to Charley's question. "I've been helping make some trail mix for the kids and some granola packets, but I don't think that's worth dinner. I have some brownies, and I thought my chili would be something that would be good if we ate outside. It is still cool."

"Carole, you're beautiful, and you didn't need to go to that much fuss. However, I love your chili, and I've got some hotdogs that will taste delicious with them covered up with all that goodness. Add some cheese, onions, and slaw, and I will think I've never eaten better. There is someone I want you to meet, and she is in the kitchen now. She will be here with me, so I would love for you to get to know her. Ali, Bob, and I met each other in college. She is here for a purpose, but you cannot ask her for what? You'll find out in time."

Carole smiled even brighter with a twinkle in her eye. "Sure! Sounds like an exciting secret!" With that, she gave a big wave to a couple of young people walking towards the hedge on the other side. "The kids are coming!"

"Hey, guys, come on over!" Charley yelled over to Bob's daughter and boyfriend. "Your dad got those burgers and dogs just about right." Charley turned to Carole and Bob and said, "I'm going to check on Ali, and we'll grab whatever is needed from inside and get started." Charley walked into the kitchen, and a few minutes later, he and Ali walked out to the gathering. "Here she is! Ali, I want you to meet everybody. I tried to warn you ahead of time there would be people joining us," Charley looked over at Ali with humor in his eyes.

Ali gave a big smile and made eye contact with everyone assembled. "Hello! It is so nice to meet everyone!"

Bob was the first to come over and brought Ali closer to where his wife was standing. "Carole, this is a friend of Charley's and mine from college."

Charley added, "We used to hang out together, although I will admit Ali and I were more serious about our studies than your husband was."

"Oh yeah, sure!" Bob defended himself quickly. recall studying intensively. Maybe my mind has gotten foggy from all those beers off-campus. Still, I remember where the library is on campus, and I think there is something like a grassy clearing where I spent a lot of time playing something, especially in November and December before the break each year.

"Okay, the library I'll give your credit for, but the green where we played softball was a no-study zone. There was serious entertainment going on there. Bob could be found there in the middle of finals every year," Charley pointed out with laughter. "Should I go on with some of my favorites? I remember when Bob…"

"We get the picture," Bob chimed in. He looked sheepishly at his daughter. "Darla, your father was much different back then, not like the very handsome and sophisticated man you have in front of you now. I am a late shiner!"

Carole had to hold back the laughter. "Ali, we are glad you are here, and I am sure that Bob will embarrass himself tonight by remembering some old stories about himself."

"This is true," Bob added. "Kids, you know your dad was just as crazy as you and your friends are now. I have to admit I was never motivated to hike a long-distance trail. However, I must let you spread your wings a bit, so I am going along with the idea. However, as he patted his pocket, I packed this baby right here. If you get in doubt or trouble, punch that speed dial number, and I am on my way."

"Wow! That sounds exciting, you two. I guess you have had some experience being outdoors before this trip to give you some practice," said Ali.

"A few short camping trips in the mountains," Darla responded. "We also went on a trip last year that Charley planned with a church group out west that allowed us to do some rafting and hiking," Darla said with youthful exuberance.

"That sounds like fun!" Ali responded. She excitedly turned to Charley and asked, "Was it Charley?"

"Yes, it was great! But Darla and all her teenage friends wore me out! I feared they would need to tie me to a mule to get me back to the parking lot. Someone else a lot younger needed to volunteer this year to chaperone a youth trip." Charley announced with laughter. "I am lying low this summer."

Ali chimed in. "There is no shame if you think you would like to stop before the end of the trail. Starting now will mean it will still be cold in those north Georgia mountains at night. Being without indoor plumbing would keep me from even starting. The sounds of the bats at night would scare me away too! I'm not sure I could do that," Ali added with a smile and merriment in her eyes as she addressed the group.

"Bats? Dad, are you going to fend off the bats if we call in the middle of the night?" Darla asked.

"Of course, Daughter. I'll wait till sunlight when the bats are all gone before I set out. But, seriously, I will come if you want to turn back or bail out anywhere. I may have half the law enforcement from several states on your trail, but we will find you." Bob turned to Ali and continued. "Carole and I have been up in the area a few times. We love the mountains. It's such a change of scenery from here in the coastal area. I've tried to talk Charley into mountain biking, but I can't convince this guy that he would not return with a broken bone."

Charley laughed again. "It's not the actual activity that scares me. The company riding in front or behind me gives me the danger sign." Moving the evening along, Charley rounded everyone up around the breezeway. "If you don't mind, I will say grace where we are all standing, and then let dinner begin."

Bob commented, "I am starving and drooling over everything. I don't want to turn into a wolf in front of everybody. However, I will take a little of this and add the chili. Then, I'll sprinkle some of this onion on top with a spot of cheese. Yes, that's looking like the best dog around."

"I'm in total agreement," said Charley as he plopped a burger on his bun and began loading it down with all the condiments and toppings. Ali looked over in amazement when he added the coleslaw before placing the bun on top to finish the stack. Charley responded with his boyish grin. "I like it with the entire farmer's garden. That's how I get my vegetable serving and keep my attractive figure!"

Ali couldn't help holding back her laughter. "I think you make a superb chef, Charley." She went to add a burger and smothered it with ketchup.

Charley teased back. He looked bewildered at her

sandwich and sarcastically commented. "Sacrilege!" and added a pickle on top of her burger.

Ali's grace with people allowed her to shine at dinner. Charley was proud of her, yet he knew others would challenge her. Would chivalry be enough to protect her from the outside world? She had been on her own, and she had bloomed. Charley thought that acceptance seemed fake if it was only on the surface. Genuine acceptance was a gift he wanted to give Ali.

Bob broke the up evening among the gathering. "We don't want to end this party early, but this clan needs to go to bed early tonight so we can make the trip to the north country tomorrow. I want to make sure that the kids make the first night out there in the wilderness before I head back. That way, if I need to bring them straight back or need something, I'm there already. We have checkpoints along the route, but I want my team to be prepared. Ali, I know Carole and I enjoyed having you with us this evening, and we hope this is the beginning of many more evenings like this one."

Ali smiled and grabbed Charley's hand. "Thank you. It has been a joy to share this evening with all of you."

The group separated, with Bob's family disappearing beyond the hedge. Finally, after the neighbors had all gone in for the night, Ali and Charley cleaned up what remained.

Charley broke the silence as he and Ali were alone in the breezeway. "Bob and Carole are close friends. As you know, Bob and I have been going back a long time. We frequently share dinner as a family. They are family. We just had different parents. I am glad you enjoyed yourself tonight. You have had a long day."

"I'm not that tired; at least, I'm not ready to go to sleep yet. It's been a magical day, and I'm not sure I want it to end just yet." Ali said.

"I see. I was going to stay up a little while myself," Charley responded. "Maybe you would like to join me for a view from the dome? There should be a superb view from up there."

Ali smiled and said, "I would love that!"

"The package I left you at Christmas. Can you find it?" Charley asked.

Ali responded with tears in her eyes. "Yes, I can find it."

"Great! I'll meet you up there in a few minutes." Then Charley went inside the house for a few minutes.

Ali went up to the studio and unzipped one of her pieces of luggage. She picked up the large envelope and waited for Charley to come up the stairs of the studio. After a while, she heard sounds outside coming closer and knew Charley must be approaching. Ali pivoted her head to watch Charley come up the ladder with the pup in one arm and a telescope in another.

"I brought Beaux along as a chaperone. I think he was getting a little lonely in the house. Go ahead of me up the stairs here, and I will give you a tour from a bird's eye view."

Ali began the ascent up the narrow spiral stairs that led up into the cupola. The dome-like area had a couple of chairs with a view that included the river and the marsh.

Charley could see the glow from the lighthouse on the next island at night. A couple of canvas chairs sat on the podium with a telescope on a stand. Charley slid the glass to the side, and a gentle breeze flowed into space through the screen. For some time, Ali and Charley sat watching the images of lights cast on the surface of the water from the moon above and the twinkling lanterns from sailboats anchored at the nearby private piers and coves. Turning to the west, she could see Savannah's skyline and its occupants bustling over roads and bridges. Charley helped Ali visualize a faint row of lights revealing a cargo ship passing through the river's mouth and out to the sea. Looking further around, the beacon from the lighthouse marked the spot where land met the ebb and flow of the ocean's tide.

Ali absorbed the beauty around her and thought back to when she had done something like this. "Sometimes, I would sit in the courtyard at the inn when no one was staying over. I would look up at the moon. I usually see the brightest star in the sky just to the moon's right, and

I contemplated who had also looked at the same star. It made me wonder if one could sense to another who looked at the same star even if they were separated centuries or miles apart?"

"Why don't you look through the telescope and see if you can find that star tonight," Charley said.

Ali moved over to look up at the indigo sky through the long cylinder. "Wow, this is amazing!" She adjusted the telescope. Ali smiled brighter and spoke out, "I found it!"

"Great!" Charley responded and then continued reaching into the box inside the package under Ali's chair. "I heard what you said at the church this afternoon, Ali."

Ali returned from the telescope and looked at the ring Charley was holding. Tears started welling up in her eyes. "I wasn't sure how you would respond. I had rehearsed my encounter with you in so many ways. I didn't have total control of what was coming out of my mouth this afternoon."

Charley took Ali's hand. "I was hoping I would have a special moment and not be on a busy street to acknowledge your response. I have held on to this ring for you for thirty years now. We can create a new one from the diamond if it does not fit anymore. I took the size of the little aquamarine ring you wore back then. We were cleaning your car one day, and you took it off and put it in the beverage holder. When you returned to the apartment for something, I made a circle so I could take it to a jeweler for the correct size on a piece of paper."

Ali put the ring on with no difficulty. "It fits Charley!" Ali paused for a moment. "It shows me you held on to hope."

"That is a discussion for another day," Charley said. He and Ali stayed up looking at the stars for some time. Eventually, the time grew into the wee hours of the morning. "It is getting late, Ali. I want you to get some sleep. But I also want you to have time to think about what you want. That is important to me. We'll talk in a few hours after we both have a good night's sleep. I know it's been a long day for you. I, for one, need all the sleep I can get to enhance my beauty!"

Ali smiled and gave him a tender kiss. "Thank you, Charley. You have made me feel cherished. You are also handsome just the way you are!"

"Perfect," Charley said and began the walk down the two flights of stairs to the studio, where Beaux was waiting for him at the door. He and his companion left Ali to her dreams.

Ali stretched on the bed, watching through the window at the night sky and feeling the comfort of the moonbeams. She felt a deep comfort within, like being soothed by a parent after reading a story before going to bed. It was such a profound gift of the heart to share tonight with others who mattered to Charley. It was like they had known her forever and valued her. Ali wanted to relive each moment again, since she had arrived every day for the rest of her life. It felt like magic. Ali wrote her thoughts down in her journal. *God, I guess you love me after all.*

Chapter 5

THE FOLLOWING DAY CAME with sounds and movement below before the sun's rising, at least above the tree line. Ali had spotted the neighbors pull out around five-thirty in the morning for their trip to the mountains, where the trailhead begins for their projected four-month hike. Ali remembered a time when she and Charley were about that age. *It was fun to be young and innocent.* She smiled over the rim of her coffee mug, sorting through her private thoughts. *That is something to enjoy for sure.* She recalled feeling that level of comfort and excitement with Charley back then. That was nice. She wrote a few pages on her laptop and was soon dazzled by the light peeping through the blinds. She also thought she heard sounds from the yard below. Ali stopped what she was doing and put on her flat so she could head down the steps. By the time she made it to the cement landing, a frisky furry friend had dashed to her and wrapped his paws around her feet. She bent down to give Beaux a hug.

"I hope we did not wake you up," Charley said. "Beaux was becoming quite impatient this morning and attempted several times to climb the stairs so he could come scratch on the door," Charley smiled. "I am glad you came down when you did. I was afraid I would have to continue listening to his mournful groan and watch his sad eyes state at me."

Ali laughed. "Beaux is used to all the attention he gets in the morning from everyone. He is quite a charmer," she patted Beaux on the head and scratched him under the chin. "Sometimes, Michael would bring him over to the inn. Beaux would curl up by the hearth in the office while I worked and never leave out a peep, even when others came and went. Then, Michael would walk through the inn, and Beaux would follow him around like a duckling."

Charley smiled and pulled a treat from his pocket, and Beaux came back to him. "Good boy!" Charley responded while placing a treat near his sneaker. "I need to win my buddy's loyalties back." Charley smiled and held out his hand to Ali. "Let us start this together. We are going to make this work, Ali. I want that very much. I want you in my life. I want Michael to be a part of my life. It is our lives, and what we choose to fill them with is our making." Soon after breakfast, Michael stopped over before catching a flight back home. Life looked good through Charley's eyes.

By the end of the week, Charley and Ali had left for some undisclosed location. Michael received instructions and followed each detail. Only a friend of Charley's had an address for finding them at a specific time and bringing the two stated witnesses. It was the exact location where Charley had planned to ask Ali to marry him thirty years ago. The sun rose over the horizon, and silver light shimmered from the rippling tide. Ancient mariner forests provided a veil of privacy. Charley and Ali finally said their vows to only the two invited individuals.

"When did you know your answer was yes?" Charley asked.

"The moment you walked with me on the shore, when we visited your parents during a school break. I was holding your hand and never wanted to let go." Ali responded.

"And you?" Ali asked.

"Let me think. Was it you who made lasagna for me the night we, no, that wasn't you? Maybe it was when we went deep-sea fishing, and no, that wasn't you either. Now I remember the day you and I decorated your sorority's float for homecoming. It must be true love if you can get a guy to do that rather than hanging out with his friends." Charley joked.

Ali posed a question as she looked deeply into Charley's dark brown eyes as he lifted the blushing veil. "Are you my warrior, Charley?"

"Yes, Ali. I am your warrior for the rest of my days."
Charley responded with no doubt in his heart.

Chapter 6

A FEW WEEKS HAD passed since that day on a quiet island away from the noisy streets of Savannah. A man stood outside the door of Charley's office at the church, looking in. "Charley, you don't have to do this. I can rotate the services with you so you don't have to be here every week."

Charley stopped for a moment. "I know. I will think about that offer seriously. I want to give Ali and me some time to focus on ourselves. I had detached myself from the direct role as a pastor in the last few years. Perhaps, I want to make this change because it is the correct change. My parents are gone. I have skills. I can work with people, but maybe differently than in the past. I'm not leaving God; I'm just stepping back from this role for a couple of months now. In my heart, a church is not an actual building. I will still serve the church, but it may be outside these walls. People have been added to my life that I never expected to ever be in my life again. The road map has changed. I will follow that sign that led me and them to me."

"Charley, I have a lot of respect for what you are doing. I wish you the absolute best. I would like you to come back after having some time to adjust to being married and having a family. You've never had that before, and it's your time. Maybe it will all lead you back here."

"Stanley, you've been a great friend, and I appreciate your words. I am ready if you'd like to help me with these boxes. I am just going to load them up. I promised someone a wedding service tomorrow in the chapel. It's a mystery, but I promised to go through with it. I normally would not have consented to this stuff, but I trust the people involved. Ali flew in tonight. I will welcome her company. She left me the RV last time she was here so we could drive back to Pennsylvania together. I am looking forward to that. We will enjoy a couple of extra days seeing the mountains and some small towns that people pass through without stopping to enjoy their beauty. Ali likes to get inspired by real people when she is traveling." Charley paused for a moment, and his eyes focused on something outside the window. "A year ago, I never mentioned her name. Now she is in my thoughts all day. Life can throw some curveballs!"

After leaving the office, Charley settled ongoing straight home and taking some quiet time to relax. Beaux was happy to have Charley's undivided attention as they walked down to the green space and onto the boardwalk that jutted out over the marsh. His prayers deepened to another layer of his being with each step he took closer to the marsh. The marsh would soon fill with the incoming tide covering the barrenness of blackish mud, left like a naked body in its shame when the tides became low.

The beauty and ugliness of nature, Charley thought for a moment. When I feel so full of life, it's like this scene at high tide, but nature ebbs and flows. *Will Ali hold my heart when life is not so perfect?* Charley was having doubts about his decision to bring Ali into his life. I'm not sure I am the warrior that Ali needs God. I am not sure I was meant for this new role. Charley contemplated in the quietness of his soul. *I need your spirit to find the path for our future.* As Charley stopped and closed his eyes at the end of the pier, he heard the water lapping against the supports beneath the walkway. In the few minutes that followed, he just stood, absorbing the essence of the water, sun, and breeze.

Ali took the same flight as CeCe and Michael to make travel arrangements easier. She had been immersed in work on the flight and had barely noticed the two-hour flight had passed. It felt strange to call Charley's place home, but Charley was kind and generous, allowing her to grow into her role as the wife of the mistress of his household. She had to admit it was a little harder for her to call the inn home with Charley. She was grateful when both of them had agreed to look for a property. That task was easy once they started spreading the word that Ali and Charley were looking for a place. Small-town communities are like that.

Michael had rented a vehicle at the airport. The plan was for CeCe and his mother to ride together to Charley's home for the weekend. It was still hard for him to get his mind around the concept of having a father. The idea got more complex when his mother and father met again and were now married. It should be every child's dream. It was more complicated in his mind and emotions. He knew them both as single adults. Now he must adjust to melting both together as one unit still. Michael stopped as he put his mother's bag in the car. "When we get to Charley's home, do I call him Dad?" he asked his mother as he closed the door on her side.

"I think, Michael, you'll know the answer when the time is right," Ali said to him with a gentle smile. "I raised you to listen to your heart. I don't think we want you to do any less."

The car turned off the main road into a more residential area. It was a quiet street with only a few houses, as the lots were larger than most on the island. Charley's car was in the drive. Michael touched the knob of the side door, and it turned. Charley was somewhere close. Ali realized Charley must be with Beaux, as no one seemed around, but the keys were sitting on the counter. Ali left Michael and CeCe in the studio above the garage with her key.

"You two settle in. I bet I know where Charley is hiding," Ali said as she walked down the steps and went down the drive. Ten minutes later, she reached the boardwalk. "Charley," Ali yelled out. She waved when she saw him spin around from the end of the pier. He began walking back to where Ali was standing. She noticed his smile first. Ali saw him just like he was when they were in college. He would smile like that when she was trying to get his attention while walking across the paved walks and shrubbery between buildings on campus—something she had forgotten about until now.

Charley kneeled and let Beaux off the leash. The puppy took off and ran straight for Ali. She waited with open arms as the furry package of energy ran for her. Ali gave Beaux a pat on his head and down along his chest, to which the pup eagerly wagged his tail and attempted to lick Ali's face. Finally, she stood up and giggled.

"Beaux, you better not get a bigger hug than me, or you're moving next door tonight!" Charley laughed.

"Now, Charley, I don't want a penalty for Beaux just because he acknowledges who spoils him the most. I promise, I am quite happy to spoil you just as much."

"That sounds like a deal! Are Michael and CeCe settled in at the house?"

"I think they are stretching their legs a bit. I opened the apartment above the garage. That gives them a bit of privacy. Besides, we still need some privacy too. I am sure they can find their way to the kitchen if they want something. We had a big brunch at the inn before we left."

"I bet you did. I miss spending time with you there. I like the idea that Michael and CeCe are so close. But I am jealous of not getting the chance to help you plow up the little herb garden out back or all those other little things you do there. But I would probably get in your hair, so time away can be a good thing."

"Yes, it makes it exciting when we are back together, though, and I am looking forward to this weekend with you and our trip to my place the long way. I was always the one that liked road trips."

"I'm not sure there will be alligators or dolphins on the way, but I think sharing some time with you would be just what I need. You were always the one to find something fun, even when there wasn't anything else to do."

"Well, I'm glad to hear that because I have no agenda for the next week except to make the two males in my life happy- Beaux and you, and perhaps not in that order." Ali laughed again and nudged Charley towards home. "Okay, partner, I need my time to beautify myself for tonight, and I'm already two hours behind my typical routine."

Charley laughed and shook his head. "Some things stay the same."

Ali looked up into his face and took his hand. It was warm and soft, and a comforting feeling seeped into her body. She matched his stride as they walked down the uneven walkway. It was a beautiful day, a wonderful feeling, and an unpredictable journey.

Michael and CeCe took up residence in the studio above the garage when Ali and Charley had returned home. Michael was the first one down the steps as he saw his parents start the drive. Michael was a 30-year-old man who made tough decisions on his job, but this moment made him nervous all day. It had frightened him even to be open to how he felt about Charley and Ali now being husband and wife. It was no longer a mother-and-son relationship. He didn't understand how the story was supposed to go, yet Michael accepted Charley as a lead character in a major part of his life now. He met them halfway and gave the couple a big smile. "Well, I guess she knew right where to find you." Michael hesitated for just a moment, and the words just flowed out. "It's good to see you, Dad!"

Charley wrapped his arms around Michael's shoulders for several seconds as he fought to keep his composure. Finally, Charley looked up and saw CeCe standing close by. He reached for CeCe's hand with his right hand and Michael's with his left. Charley's eyes beamed. "I am happy to have you both here! It looks like Ali's set you up in the studio, which should be perfect for giving you two some privacy. Ali and I want you to enjoy being wherever you want to be. CeCe, what about your parents? I am assuming they have plans?"

"Yes, my parents are in the area already. They had so many things on their lists to do that they told us not to worry about them until we see them at dinner tonight with all of you. I texted Mother when we arrived, and she said all was going smoothly. She passed on the message from Steven that he has taken care of everything, and he is looking forward to seeing you again, Charley."

Charley looked somewhat puzzled. "Have I met your brother before CeCe? He said nothing about that when we spoke on the phone."

"Well, I guess he thinks he's met you?" CeCe smiled back. "I do not know more than that."

Michael quickly shrugged as Charley opened his mouth to ask him the same question.

"Well, this is a mystery, but I'm getting a vibe here. I guess I will have to wait until this evening."

Michael took CeCe's arm and began moving towards the garage steps. "Oh, and by the way, CeCe and I decided we will call you both Mother and Dad from here on out. We want to be clear it was a unanimous decision! We'll see you two love birds later!" Michael and CeCe laughed as they climbed the stairs to the studio.

Charley responded with a grin and looked back at Ali. "Okay, now that we've settled on that, we can start on the next situation. What I would like to do right now is grab some iced tea and relax a bit. After that, anyone who wants to join me on the patio can," Charley yelled out so that occupants at the top of the steps could hear. "There are more choices in the kitchen fridge. Help yourself to whatever meets your fancy. Beaux and I have simple likes. Give us a place to close our eyes, and we will curl up and relax, right, buddy?" Charley bent down, rubbed Beaux's chin, and laid a treat on the ground. "As for you, Ali, you are welcome to join me on this fine day or rest inside, where it is less humid."

Ali followed Charley into the kitchen and grabbed sparkling water from the fridge and the pitcher full of tea. She gently touched his cheek and whispered something in his ear.

Charley looked at Ali and blushed while he smiled. "So that's the way it's going to be. You have got your wish, Mrs. Howard." He laughed a little more and shook his head. After grabbing a couple of mugs and pouring the beverages into each container, he walked through the French door. "Let's soak in some Vitamin D together on the patio first. Maybe we can cause a stir in the neighborhood."

Ali followed him and settled down on the lounger next to Charley. Thirty minutes later, Ali stood by the kitchen window and looked at the man she had married just two months earlier. *How did this crazy thing happen? Where was he all those years?* Ali felt a comforting thought pass through her mind, and it remaindered her that God was with her. She glanced at the natural beauty through the window and felt the moment. Ali walked back to the bedroom to finish dressing. She faintly heard her husband singing a song when he walked into the kitchen that they both knew very well from their college years. It was a private pleasure, with no guilt involved.

Charley was ready in under thirty minutes. He rounded up the other occupants at five-thirty, and the car was rolling down the street by five-thirty-five. The wedding couple requested that there be no need for a formal rehearsal this evening as the wedding would be family. The host and hostess invited Reverend and Ali Howard to a dinner party at a local establishment, as stated on the invitation. Michael and CeCe were preparing for the evening to celebrate the marriage of CeCe's brother, Steven, and his bride-to-be. At six, the sedan turned onto a less congested street and found a spot to parallel park along the narrow side street. The location for this celebration was a restaurant on the fringe of the historic district. The old mansion had been converted into an upscale restaurant several years ago. It was a delight to the locals. Hydrangeas flanked the wrap-around porch with daylilies, adding splashes of color in the sunny locations of the lawn. Impatiens nestled under the shade of the trees in front. On each side of the entrance door were two large baskets on pedestals, each holding a large fern. Charley glimpsed a young man in a wheelchair with a young lady being escorted onto the side porch when they arrived. A passing thought entered Charley's head, but he threw the idea off as he took Ali's hand. He welcomed her comforting squeeze from her hand, letting him know she was a part of his life. A group came out of the entrance, which included Richard and Rona, along with another couple. CeCe's father was the first to take a leap down the stairs and give his daughter- and son-in-law a big hug. Richard reached out to Ali as well.

"Well, here you are! We are so happy to have everyone with us tonight." Richard smiled at Charley. "Rona and I want to tell you how pleased that you and Ali found each other after all these years and got married. Welcome to our extended family! We all were delighted for you both!"

"Richard tells the truth. We were both thrilled to hear the news!" Rona chimed in. "However, I must confess, I think the tears of joy were more from one of those hot peppers he put on the veggie burger he ate when he got the news." Rona smiled back and rubbed a bit of lipstick from his neck. "Okay, Richard, will you let me hug the newlyweds?" Rona burst out as she gave Charley and Ali both a hug. Then, turning to Maggie's parents, Richard introduced Maggie's parents to the Howards. "Delbert and Marie Hess are Maggie's parents. Maggie's their only daughter."

Charley smiled and reached out to greet Marie and Delbert. "I am delighted to meet you. My wife and I welcome you to Savannah. Where are you from?"

"Thank you, Reverend Howard. We are enjoying the trip so far. We live in San Antonio. I knew of Savannah from my days in the military thirty years ago. Marie has never been east of the Mississippi, so this is a treat for us!"

"Please call me Charley. This is my wife, Ali. Michael is our son and is married to Steven's sister."

"Yes, I have heard so much about you. Steven and Michael are close friends. We are incredibly pleased to meet you." exclaimed Marie.

"I am so glad to share this special time with Steven and Maggie," said Ali, as she smiled warmly at both families. "When did you arrive in town?"

"We came on Thursday morning. We haven't stopped since we landed, enjoying seeing the beautiful coast. We wanted to visit more, but we just could not put it in our schedule," responded Mrs. Hess.

"Yes, there are some lovely places to visit," Ali shared with Maggie's parents. "Charley and I married on an island off the Georgia coast. It is a special place for us. I hope you will come back again and visit us. Charley and I would love to have you spend a week with us. We are now trying to split our lives between my home in Pennsylvania, where I have an inn and restaurant, and Charley's home here."

"Absolutely!" Charley added.

Soon a host greeted the group and ushered them

along the porch through an iron gate that led to a courtyard and a smaller building that was probably once a stable or unattached garage.

Ali took in the beautiful sight of glass orbs with candles placed on side tables around the fountain in the courtyard. The pulse of the water from the fountain provided a symphony of relaxing and peaceful sounds. The double doors from the smaller building were wide open, allowing a golden light from a large chandelier to flood the courtyard with a soft glow. A whiff of savory aromas penetrated the evening air. Ali looked at Charley, and he looked back. She thought there was a depth in those eyes, layers of life experiences. She had loved the young man when he was starting life, but now there was a depth about him that was a mystery. How would they be merged again as a committed partnership for this stage in their life? Ali and Charley smiled and followed the group to the courtyard. In the courtyard was a man sitting in a wheelchair with a young woman beside him.

"Hello, everyone, and welcome." The man greeted everyone with a big smile on his face.

Richard was the first to walk over to the young man and place his hands on both shoulders, smiling back at the guests. "My son Steven and his bride-to-be, Maggie, are our honored guests this evening. Most of us have met, but for Maggie's benefit, I will introduce you to Michael's parents, Reverend Charles and Ali Howard. Reverend Howard and Steven met some time ago. We are saving the story later in the evening."

Charley didn't question the groom, but he recalled from the conversation in Pennsylvania that they had met in the past. He continued to have a smile on his face as he greeted everyone. His mind was sorting through chads of memories from the past. His mind was pulling up a memory of his past. He kept the memory to himself. He turned again to the woman who came with him tonight. As a diamond sparkles in the moonlight, Ali sparkled on Charley's arm with her elegant mannerisms and graceful charm. Both easily connected with other guests with their warm personalities and calm demeanor.

Steven grasped Maggie's hand. "We planned this destination wedding keeping things simple but surrounded by those who mean the most to us. We will allow the servers to finish up in the private room next door and begin dinner in twenty minutes. In the meantime, please walk to the tables where there are foods to nibble on and cold drinks. I talked Dad out of having a zydeco band tonight," Steven joked. "But I think I saw sand thrown on the ground this evening when no one was looking. Could be a bag came on the plane with someone from Breaux Bridge."

Richard laughed. "Could have been someone with some sand in their flip-flops trying out moves on the dance floor earlier. Who knows?" He returned the joke with a wink to everyone.

Steven laughed at his father, although he knew

nothing was too impossible for Richard. His practical jokes were getting a little more elaborate with age. Steven continued. "With some help from some friends, Maggie and I put this brief presentation together to tell our love story."

A white tent with white and gold fabrics draped from the ceiling to each corner of the tent, appearing like ribbons, had been placed in the courtyard. In addition, lanterns had been placed to give the space a shimmering light. The guests gathered under the tent with chairs around a large screen where the video started. There were family stories and shots of Steven and Maggie growing up. Edited in the storylines were comments from various individuals telling the story from childhood until the present.

Charley laughed and smiled as the others watched the scenes. There was humor on CeCe's side of the family. Next, the background music shifted in intensity, and then there were scenes of Steven in a rehab center, his father making videos of Steven working with his therapist, Maggie. Next, there were scenes of hive fives and tears. Eventually, the scenes moved on to handholding and dates of fun and romance as everyone in the group laughed and watched the video with tears of joy and laughter at the antics. One person in the group fell silent with eyes closed, tears running down his face, yet his lips smiled. Michael pulled his chair closer to Charley's chair. Ali was also aware of Charley's expression and knew that there was a hidden story. At the end of the presentation, everyone clapped and cheered.

Steven raised his hand to speak. I hope everyone enjoyed our video about Maggie and me and how we started our relationship. "It took a lot of time to sit down, go through the interviews and edit the scenes," Steven joked. It cost me many beers and muffulettas to get all the people we knew and the scenes we wanted. At dinner, we wanted to share a bit more of the story. I see the signal that they are ready for us so that we can move on to the dining area. Thanks to Maggie and our two mothers who worked so hard today to make it memorable. They would not allow me around all day. Dad, Delbert, and I had to fend for ourselves." Maggie laughed and patted Steven's cheek.

"But we managed, didn't we guys?" Steven added.

"Yes, we took advantage of the time we had! It took us five minutes to make a beeline, grab some fishing rods and lawn chairs, and head out to the pier," Richard happily added. "We did not care if there was anything to catch or not. We just watched the scene go by." Richard stood by Steven's chair and motioned for Steven to wheel himself into the dining room to maneuver around the space accessible by the wheelchair. Maggie's parents followed Maggie.

Charley took his wife's hand but allowed Ali to lead. They found their name cards next to one another and sat down. Once all found their way around the table. Servers came to provide beverages and plates of low-country cuisine. Then, dinner began with a simple grace said and a toast from the bride's father.

Ali was at her best tonight, being with whom she came to know as family. Bloodlines or not, these were the people she loved the most. Ali genuinely felt the joy of Steven and his bride-to-be. She knew the feeling of pride and grief of raising a son only to release him into the embrace of his soulmate. She could empathize with the sparkle of moisture that pooled in Rona's eyes now and then as she looked over at Steven. Ali remembered holding back tears when Michael came to this moment in his life. Her mother's heart sadly let go that day so he could grow as a husband. The faces around the table had brought so much pleasure into Ali's life, just like creole seasoning in gumbo.

Steven tapped his glass. "It is time that the story continues as I promised." Steven looked down at the table where Michael's father was sitting. "Reverend Howard, do you remember me now?"

Charley smiled with a humble nod. " I remember, Steven." Charley quickly flashed a bashful smile and dug into his lemon pie to avoid answering further questions. Memories flooded him, and he was barely holding back the tears.

Ali, too, was quiet, but her mind was dancing with intrigue. While she sipped on champagne, her cheeks felt warm, and her hand took a bit of an adventure to touch the soft curls brushing the collar of her husband's shirt for just a moment before she felt a joyful fuzzy feeling coming over her. She used a napkin to cover her mouth as a bit of a giggle gently left her lips.

Charley swallowed and put his hand up to his mouth. He then looked at Ali with her sparkling eyes. "Steven, I am honored to be your guest this evening. As I think, I know where your story is leading. May I draw the attention back to you and your lovely wife-to-be? Just as I met Ali at the junction of my life's journey, not once but twice through a miracle of faith, you have found your love. I am humbled to have met you and assisted you. I suspect you had a role in bringing my son and Ali into my life again. If I say anything more, we will need a boat to reach our cars out on the street from all my tears of gratitude."

Richard chimed in. "Rona and I are indebted to you for finding our son with his broken body that night and not leaving him until we could get here the next day. We did not want to say anything at Christmas, but we've known about you for some time, Charley. You are in the family now.

Charley grinned big and nodded.

Steven took the conversation back. "Let me share this story about how CeCe and Michael met. He probably did not tell you this part. After I went through a rehabilitation period and needed to work for my sanity, I started working for Dad's company after the accident, just a few days at first, and then I kept building more time in my work week. Soon after returning, I made a new friend with one of the up-and-coming engineers. One day, he tricks me into introducing him to this girl at the office. I thought it was funny when he went on and on about this girl he met in the elevator. Once he described her to me, I knew it was CeCe. He asked me if I knew her. CeCe did not come in much, but she would do little favors for me. He thought she was someone outside the company who assisted me because of my injury. He was not wrong about that assumption. I never told him otherwise. I led one. I knew her well and even had a way to contact her if he wanted to follow up and ask her out. I intentionally gave him Dad's number to contact her. I let Dad in on it ahead of time. Dad is a good sport about most things, so he went along with it."

Richard added, "I had the best time on that phone call. I could hardly contain myself. Michael figured out who I was within the first few minutes. You could tell, and I knew he was sweating to end the call. Eventually, I had to give the boy some rope and turned over the phone to CeCe, who was at home with us for dinner."

CeCe further told her side of the event. "Dad, I will never forget that night. I did not know Michael was going to call. Steven said something to me earlier in the day about joining him and Maggie with a friend on Saturday for low-key pizza. With Steven, you never know who you will meet, so I said sure. I didn't know it was the guy from the elevator. I thought he was cute the day I stopped to talk to him on the way up to Steven's office. I knew he was probably one of Dad's employees. I told myself she was off-limits. I was in college, and I had a lot of other things on my mind. The exams for my mass media and business law classes were coming up on Monday, and the meeting for the sorority float for homecoming weekend was Saturday morning. My calendar notes the important stuff in my life! If I went out on a blind date with a guy lined up by my brother and approved by my father, it better be worth it. I didn't always trust these two characters," with CeCe looking at Richard and her brother Steven. "I cannot tell you the visions I had in my head all morning while I was folding and pulling apart yellow and purple tissue paper for carnations; however, because of my deep love for my dear, sweet brother. I put my best foot forward that evening. All I can say was that it was love at first bite at Gio's Pizzeria!" Laughter flowed around the table.

CeCe's mother added, "I don't think poor Michael had a chance after that first date. He may have thought he was the pursuer, but I can tell you CeCe wasn't planning to throw that fish back in the water!"

"I concur. CeCe's just like her mother. When she knows she has found the best, she reels him in fast," Richard teased and finished a wink in his wife's direction.

Ali and Charley soaked in all the banter and laughter from the guests at the table. There was a richness in the storytelling between friends and family when all came together for weddings and funerals.

Steven patted Michael on the back and continued the story. "CeCe got married to Michael. Michael told me things about his life. I met Michael's lovely mother, Ali. She was talented, beautiful, and successful. What is not to love about Ali? I told myself. Michael's father was a mystery. Michael described him in positive terms. One day, as I was working on something, Savannah flashed into my mind. It was like being hit by a beam from the light of a lighthouse. Then Dad told me about an issue the company needed to address in the plant here. Michael told me he was taking CeCe to the Georgia coast for their anniversary a few days later. Dad and I had a conversation before Michael and CeCe's departure. I had dropped a few hints with Michael to check on something if he had the opportunity. My purpose was only to make the connection. Fate would have its way. That night you told me if you had a son, you would never have left him, so you would not leave me until my father came. I believed you, Charley."

Ali's eyes shined in the candlelight, and Charley noticed when he turned to look at her.

Maggie's father put his arm around her mother, and his daughter was pleased by the surprise of her father's show of affection. Maggie wiped a tear away from her eyes. The table became quiet, but smiles were seen on several faces as Steven took the continued the story he began at the beginning of the evening.

"Maggie, do you want to share now?"

"Well, first, we want to say that we love all of you here this evening. Mom and Dad, you've been my foundation for what I want my family to be. Rona and Richard, you are my new family, and you gave me Steven, so how could I not love you? Michael, you are Steven's best friend, and CeCe, you have become mine. Charley and Ali, you have created a love story of faith that Steven and I want to do the same. We love all of you and wanted you all to be part of our celebration, though we wanted to keep things simple."

As the night progressed with ease, Steven had arranged for entertainment with ghost stories of the old port city told by an actor around the glowing lanterns. Charley had grown up hearing many of the tales shared. However, watching the flickering lights from the firepit seemed possible in the evening ambiance.

Long after the evening activities were over and the families had left for their destinations for the night, Charley and Ali were still sitting on the patio with a mosquito net tented around them as they spoke intimately to each other for several hours more. It was an evening they wanted to savor.

Upstairs in the studio, no lights were on. Instead, whispers flowed between the bed partners. "What do you think your mother and Charley are talking about down there?"

"It's hard to tell, maybe asking who will pay the

electric bill this month." Michael smiled back at his wife.

"You know better than that. Ali and Charley wouldn't stay outside on the patio talking all night unless they're talking about important things."

"That's probably true," Michael responded. Then, feeling sleepy, he immediately shut his eyes and drifted to sleep.

"What important things are they saying?" CeCe asked teasingly.

"CeCe, I have come to the belief that I came from a gene pool of two brilliant, faithful people who have learned to live life not as expected, but it turned out to be. I suppose they are just comparing notes."

"You are impossible!"

"Yes, that is one of my God-given natural traits. I'm fond of that one." Michael responded, then kissed her forehead and bid her good night.

In the morning, a new day arrived. Steven and Maggie were married quietly in the old chapel on Saturday and left with a sense of sublime simplicity as quietly as they came. They said their goodbyes tearfully and rolled out of the parking lot and onto the main street. Soon it would be Michael's and CeCe's turn to fly away like snowbirds on their annual return to their habitat. Unfortunately, Ali would leave as well to handle her business affairs. Charley would follow in just a week. His old nature spoke a different message, but his desire to move forward was clear. He wanted to be with those he loved more dearly than anything he would leave behind. Perhaps the stay would not be forever. In the real world, no one knows where the adventure leads. He saw himself as a ship in the harbor waiting to sail.

Chapter 7

IT HAD BEEN FOUR days since the wedding. Three days were left until Charley would make his departure. Charley made directions for tasks. After packing and shipping some items to Pennsylvania, Charley took a long break. With Beaux in tow, he drove to the old neighborhood where he had grown up. Charley found a parking spot a couple of blocks away and walked the final distance to his parent's old home, the one Charley sold a few years back to free himself of memories. Impressions are the word he would use to describe his life growing up in that house. Charley grew up and experienced life outside the walls. He knew impressions were mainly made up of the character of the world around him. Therefore, he loosened the ties of the others' impressions they had tried to impose on him. Beaux trotted along his side, taking an occasional sniff under the canopy of tree branches and moss. An occasional acquaintance yelled out a greeting. Charley stopped for a few minutes to chat. He continued his walk, not allowing Beaux to get too impatient. He passed the homes of several families he had known. Many of the houses bought by newcomers were children from a previous generation. Life renewed itself in stages, Charley thought as he walked down the sidewalk. Most people hid in the warm, humid afternoon air, where the air conditioning, fans, and high-ceiling rooms made it more comfortable. He looked at the white stucco home ahead of him for a few moments. It had all the right things, a giant magnolia tree on the side with oaks in the front yard shading the lawn from the hot summer temperatures. The house showed a sun porch in the back that was the entire length of the house. Flagstone and gravel marked the path along the home's outer edge, connecting the front yard to the rear along a trail of hydrangea and boxwoods. Charley knew he would miss being so far away. Closing his eyes, he took a moment and fought back conflicting views. Charley, with simple courage, pushed aside his doubts and fears. Faith took the path of letting go and finding oneself along the way home. Charley looked down at Beaux and laughed. "I don't know about you, Beaux, but I think we need to find a local watering hole fast!" Charles and Beaux found their way back in half the time. Charley made his last stop before returning home. Goodbyes, even for a brief time, we're always bittersweet.

Saturday finally arrived, and Charley had plans to

pull out by eight. At seven in the morning, the neighbors were up and stirring outside. Charley had taken Beaux for his long walk and completed the tasks before pulling out.

"I've got you covered, Charley," Frogman responded. "You will be back in a few months. It will feel good to get out of this heat for a while. Take your time settling in up there and then find out what it is like not to be a bachelor anymore. Keep your place here until you are sure you are not coming back."

Charley just laughed and shook his head. "You know, we could get this done faster if you helped me load these boxes."

"Of course. Tell me what needs to go next."

"That chair could go right here, and I could tie it down, so it won't move," Charley told Frogman as they moved the chair inside the trailer and covered it. Then they tied it down to protect it during the trip.

"Is this another one of those you made, Charley? I haven't seen this before?"

"Yes, I made one for Ali to take on this trip, and I shipped one to Michael's home the other day. I can get this one up there before Michael's chair arrives."

Bob asked, "Does Ali know who makes this stuff?"

"Not really. There is no real reason to hide it from her, and I will tell her soon enough, but it hasn't come up in discussion. She saw the work I put into the loft and knows I like to work with my hands. I like to keep some pieces of my life private, Bob."

"That you do! You sure have had some wonderful chapters in your life lately. I don't know how you do it! I thought I knew you like a brother and discovered you are just never run out of surprises."

"Not really. I cannot create a storyline about my life. It just happens." Charley heard footsteps behind him as he stepped away from the motorized home with items loaded for Pennsylvania. He turned around and wiped the sweat that was forming on his forehead. He sincerely appreciated friends as he saw Carole coming with a cooler.

"Charley, I have packed you and Beaux some snacks so that you don't have to unpack anything when you stop to take a break. I even made a gallon of fresh tea with a bag of ice so you can sip some later in the day. Of course, it would be best to have no withdrawal symptoms while driving. We are thinking of Beaux's protection, of course. Your meanness comes out when you're running low on the stuff."

"Thank you. I know your heart is in the right place," Charley said and hugged his neighbor. "That is sweet of you." Charley picked up the cooler she put at his feet. "I think this is about everything. If I bring anything more, I will have to leave Beaux here. If I arrive without him, I am afraid Ali would leave me and return for him. Right, Beaux?" Charley patted the furry creature with a soft touch. "Beaux, it is time to head on out and meet your sister along with a pretty lady who's waiting on you." Charley opened the door to let the prancing puppy in the passenger side and followed in on his own.

Bob stood on the vehicle's passenger side, gesturing for Charley to roll the window down. "You know Charley, it's just a thought, but you could convince her to live here. It is not unheard of for the man's wife to move where her husband lives and works. We miss Ali and Beaux already, and his four paws here haven't even left drive." Bob placed a hand underneath Beaux's nose and gave him a treat. He then put the box back in a bag and set it behind Beaux's seat.

Charley shook his head. "You know this pooch gets more love than I do."

"Well yeah! Beaux's just a puppy torn between two families who love him. He doesn't know what's happening to him tossed around, do you, Beaux? You think you are off for a frisbee game on the beach, and your owner takes you off to some small unknown town far away from where it's gray from October through May. Beaux, be brave. Somebody has your back here in the land of sweet peaches and Palmetto bugs."

"You are laying it thick, Bob, but it's not going to work." Charley laughed. "Well, I guess this is it for a while. I will let you know my plans as I get settled.

You know how to reach me for anything. I cannot tell you how much I appreciate all that you have done! You are my family where it counts," Charley pointed to his heart. Pulling out of the drive, he waved back before backing out onto the street. Charley set his gaze forward, eyes shuttered by his sunglasses. His directions were simple as he started on the next track of his life.

Chapter 8

ALI WAS BUSY, TRYING to finish up the last of the entries for the day. Charley was on his way home and arriving soon based on his last text. That felt very good to her. She last spoke to him while Charley was in Virginia, basking in mountain views and following bears, or were they following him? Charley wanted to watch the sunrise with Beaux, according to his account. She could visualize him with his morning stubble and salt and pepper hair naturally falling into soft waves. She could feel the soft, long-sleeved jersey he would wear in the early morning hours. Charley wore the same when he took Beaux for the early morning walk down to the pier. She laughed to herself. These little tidbits she had already learned about him. Yet there was so much more to see beyond the flesh. Around four o'clock, someone knocked on her office door. "Come in," Ali spoke as she stretchered her neck and shoulders.

"Ali, there's a man here that says he has something to deliver but needs you to sign specifically," said the familiar voice of the inn's manager.

"Okay, I will be right there." Ali glanced out the window, looking baffled, and then smiled. She quickly checked her makeup in the mirror on the mantle, ensured everything was in place, and proceeded to the front parlor. Ali looked around, but only a few patrons were sitting in the front room dining, enjoying their meal. She looked quizzically at the staff. Finally, a server spoke up and showed that the delivery was at the service door.

"I see, thank you," Ali replied as she walked faster through the kitchen, into the pantry area, and to the side door. As she opened the door, a man with dark glasses and a hat stood with a clipboard.

"I need a signature, please, before I can leave this. My instructions clearly say to match the name to the one provided by the sender."

"Is that right?" Ali questioned, then walked closer to the man.

"That's right. I can only give this to one lady; the name must match."

"Oh, really?" Ali smiled back. She wrote a name on the form and looked quizzically at her naughty self.

"Sorry, ma'am, that does not match. She queen died sometime around 400 BC. Is there another lady at the inn?"

"Let me try again." Ali wrote something else down on the clipboard, holding back her giggles.

"Thank you, Mrs. Howard. I am to give you this when you answer correctly."

Ali looked at the large shipping crate on the dolly. "Wow! This is so exciting!" She tried to figure out the contents. She wondered what it could be as she put her hands on the wood crate and felt around its width and length?

"Be careful, lady. The contents in the box are very fragile. However, it arrived with special instructions to handle it with much care. I think the sender even included gentle loving care."

"Thank you. I usually am not this forward with a delivery man, and I hope I do not get you in trouble with your boss," Ali said in a low-volume voice as she turned around to see who was listening. She whispered in his ear. "I think you are the most handsome delivery man I have ever seen, Charley."

Later that evening, Beaux lounged on the floor with Ali rubbing his back. Charley was putting up the mirror above the mantel.

"That is a perfect spot. The mirror frame is simple, but the wood stain is unique. Charley, you have such an eye for artistry with your hands. I think you missed your calling."

Charley smiled back. "Thank you. I work on things that I want to make. I am a teacher, preacher, and carpenter, but I never was a songwriter or storyteller. That is your area of expertise. I live for my next pleasure like biscuits and back rubs, right Beaux?" Beaux perked up his ears, then slowly closed his eyes again and nestled back in peaceful rest. "I wanted to bring you something. I thought of the night I first saw you again on Christmas Eve with your reflection in the mirror. I tried to capture that moment. I can make things with my hand, and I came up with this idea." Charley stepped down the ladder and looked up at what his hand had created.

"The mirror looks lovely there," Ali responded, and kissed Charley.

The next day, a box was waiting at the inn's service door when Ali came out at noon. Ali waited until Charley came home for the day and called him over to her office.

Charley knocked before entering as if he was one of the staff. When he entered, Ali jumped up from her desk and pointed to the box that had arrived earlier. "This crate came earlier today marked: Attention Owner of the Inn. I had to peek. I've been waiting for you ever since." Ali said excitedly.

"Do you like it?" Charley asked.

"This chair is perfection." Ali walked over and placed her hands on the bow back spindles. "These are hand carved. Charley, I never saw you do any furniture when I was in Savannah. How did you learn to do this kind of work?"

Charley diverted his gaze for just a moment to breathe in and out. "I am self-taught with some help from a few other talented guys. There's a place where I go to work, sometimes away from the downtown area. It's a place where I can hang out and be myself. I worked on it there so you wouldn't find it by accident." Charles added in a quiet voice. "You used to like things I made you."

Ali looked closely into his face. "I do. The chair goes beyond all those wooden boxes and shelves I saw. She looked at the fine lines around his eyes and tenderly touched the soft stubble along his cheeks and jaw. "Charley, are you hiding something from me?"

Without answering, Charley moved slightly away. As requested, Charley positioned the chair near the stone hearth in the back parlor. He admired the piece in the setting, thinking it was a good fit.

The scene was just as Ali pictured it years ago when she typed her first story. She remembered what she felt and included it in the storyline about the stone hearth. Then, Ali's mind drifted to a more recent memory of herself opening the envelope that Charley had placed in her hands on the day he left in December. There was the story she had written and had given Charley that Christmas break as a gift long ago. Also, inside the envelope were a small box and a card. The card went with the engagement ring that Charley had stored away after that painful day. The card explained Charley's intentions in asking Ali to be his wife and that he would wait until she was ready to say yes. Charley had written the note that morning before he had gone to play golf with his dad. That same day, Ali ran far away from the hurtful words she heard from his mother in that pristine living room where Mrs. Howard enshrined her family's heirlooms. Unfair and rejecting words felt like wasps stinging Ali's entire body that day. Ali had gathered her things and left before Charley had made it back. She left a note to Charley on his bed saying she had gone and that she had decided that it was best to end the relationship. No comment about where she was going, only that she had a ride to the airport. Tears flowed as Ali was brought back to the present. She tenderly let her hand reach out to Charley's face.

"I thought it would make you feel at home while you're sitting near the fire," Charley responded.

"I am at home wherever you are, Charley."

"I thought the chair would make you happy," Charley replied, but questioned Ali's response with tears.

"It doesn't make me happy, Charley. It is a beautiful gift. I want to keep it here by the fireplace for now. It will remind me of you when I am in my world—oh, speaking of my world. I got this call earlier today from Reverend Collins. He wanted to speak to you, thinking you might be here already. He asked if I would give you his contact information and for you to call him at your leisure."

"I wonder what that call had to do with me. I will follow up tomorrow and see." After several more hours of talking and relaxing, the lights turned off at the inn. Before turning his head away from the pillow that night, Charley kissed Ali on the nose. "It's been a long journey for both of us." He quickly nodded off to sleep while looking forward to the morning.

The next day, Charley was up early, bringing a large mug of hot coffee down to the barn. He climbed up the barn ladder to sit on a box on a hayloft's floor. He allowed this to be his quiet time. No one would look for him here in the barn. With a little improvising, he made a little table and pulled out a notepad and pen. Then he pulled a small book from another pocket inside his old vest. It was the same vest he wore in the workroom in Savannah. A couple of hours later, Charley appeared at the service door with a crate of fruits and vegetables he had picked up at a farmers' market in a small village north of Winchester. He brought them in for the kitchen manager, who was already busy preparing food for the day.

"Well, Reverend Howard, you have made my day. I will not have to have someone go off to the closest grocery store now. I can see from here something I can use for the side dishes and maybe an extra appetizer or two as a special treat," replied Hazel.

"Great idea! I loved your cooking, as I recall from Christmas."

"Well, I'd not be humble enough if I didn't say Ali made most of the dinner that evening. But make a fantastic citrus spinach salad. I will send up to the apartment for you and Ali to have for lunch today. I think Ali was thinking of Michael and CeCe coming over and having dinner on the patio tonight. Maybe I will save that one for dinner tonight and fix some squash with something else for a light lunch. I see the potential in this crate."

"I will love anything you fix, but Ali and I can fend for ourselves, I'm sure. I make a mean peanut butter and jelly with bacon, but I will dive into a great salad any day."

"Bologna and mayonnaise with a fresh slice of tomato and lettuce on toast is my favorite for Saturday." Mrs. Casey responded with humor.

"You know a man's heart, Hazel," Charley said with a smile. "I'm sure Ali will be pleased with whatever you both decide. Is Ali in her office?"

"I believe so."

Charley took the back hall to Ali's office. Instead of going inside, he scribbled some notes on a piece of paper, placed a smiley face on the other side, folded it, and slid it under her door. *She could find it when she got up to walk around the room, and I wouldn't disturb her.* After a quick cleanup, Charley headed to a town about thirty minutes away. He was unsure what this meeting was about, but Charley agreed to meet Reverend Collins after speaking to him early this morning. He found his destination with a bit of help from technology. Charley walked up to a neatly landscaped pre-fabricated building marked with a sign for the office. He rang the doorbell, and a pleasant voice greeted him through the intercom. Charley gave his name, and he was warmly welcomed and asked to come inside.

"Good morning, Reverend Howard. I am Mrs. Scott, the church secretary. We usually have people come in freely all day long. The doorbell is for Saturdays or evenings when someone is alone, and they are a little nervous about having the front door open when there is no one at the desk. I will let them know you have arrived."

"Thank you," Charley replied. Less than five minutes had passed when a man in his early thirties came to greet Charley.

"Reverend Howard, I am Reverend Jason Collins. I am happy you could come in today. I am the Youth Pastor here. Mr. Rowlands is on the Board of Directors here. I will tell you more than we walk over to the church." After meeting Mr. Rowlands and passing a few general pleasantries, Reverend Collins directed the group to the church sanctuary next door.

Charley felt somewhat neutral about this entire conversation, as this was not on his radar when he left Savannah.

The men sat down on the chairs in the front and second rows. Reverend Collins began his request. "Dr. Joseph Collins, my father, has been the pastor at this church for over twenty-five years. Unfortunately, he is not here as he has begun his radiation therapy today for a brain tumor that was recently diagnosed. We know now that it is a fast-growing tumor and not prognostically favorable. My father knows he will not preach again. My father wishes to find a temporary replacement immediately. A search for a permanent pastor is underway. My father and I have spoken to each other on the matter. More than one source in the ministry brought your name to our attention. We understand that you have just been married and have recently left Savannah, at least for a brief period, to join your wife, who lives in the area."

With a stoic expression, Charley sat and listened as both men spoke. Finally, Charley soberly responded to their proposal. "I am sorry for your father's condition and the stress you must be feeling right now. All that you have said about me so far is true. I have not decided if I will return to Savannah in the fall. I still have some other business there that does not relate to my position as a pastor, so my time spent back and forth is to be determined."

The younger man went on with the discussion. "I was a little concerned about that. Your name came from a mutual acquaintance, Stanley Fox. We know you have strong ties to the church there. If I may be candid with all of us here, my father has requested that you consider this temporary role for the next four to eight weeks. He also suggested that you come by between nine and ten tomorrow morning to his home. He receives medication at eleven, which clouds his thinking afterward."

Charley looked into the eyes of the son with a comforting expression. "I will be happy to visit with your father tomorrow. You can email the details of the location. Here is my card. Regardless of my decision, I will do that for your father. Let me think about this and decide with some prayer." That concluded the discussion, and Charley was free to do the rest of the day's business. Charley made a few more stops after his first visit of the day. He accomplished most of the things on his checklist. Charley visited a local barber to clean up his mass of curls that transitioned from a tickle sensation to a continuous scratchy feeling at the base of his neck. He dropped off a package for shipment. Charley then traveled back to the inn. Taking the private entrance, he could walk to the owner's quarters with minimal distraction from anyone. Charley didn't want to talk anymore, and some privacy would be enjoyable. But, of course, Beaux and Bea received their due attention when he made his presence known. He remembered dinner tonight with Michael and CeCe, but Charley was sure Ali could keep things going if he faded. And so, it was dinner on the side porch with Beaux and his new best friend nibbling from their dishes, made specially for the two canines. There was easy cleanup tonight with paper plates and plastic utensils to match the picnic-style dinner Ali had put together. With everyone giving a hand, the table returned to its normal state. The remaining leftovers on the table had been whisked away into the kitchen.

Charley sat down in a soft patio chair with Beaux lying at his feet on the ottoman. He looked around at everyone. Life is not what you think it will sometimes be, he thought to himself. Hope isn't always easy to hang on to when one's deepest wishes don't come the way one wanted. Charley knew the darker times of life. He wanted to enjoy the good times of life like this evening. His tent was full of family, and love had grown over the last year. That was riches to Charley.

"Charley, you've been very busy today. Is there anything you want to share?" Ali asked as they all sat watching the sunset over the hilltops.

"Not right now. I have some things that are on my mind this evening. I'm not ready to talk about it just yet. Maybe by tomorrow, I will have more things to say. Today, I found that the best unsweetened iced tea is made at the little coffee shop near the college."

"Oh... Who's my competition?" Ali looked at her husband with narrow eyes but glee in her tone of voice.

Charley bantered back. "I knew I was going to get heat on this one! I must explain that they serve it in a tall, extra-large plastic container with your choice of any college or university logo on it. For an extra charge, you can make it a to-go cup. There are two examples in the cabinet above the sink right now."

"For goodness's sake!" Ali exclaimed, followed by laughter. "Did you find one from our alma mater?"

Charley grinned and shook his head, affirming what he had just said.

"Wow! You know I have never been there. It opened right before football season last year. I always thought of it as a college hangout, so I never to stop in," Ali responded.

CeCe added, "I usually don't stop. However, we sometimes attend some college activities, so stopping before or after an event is nice. It is more than you might think. They have a section where people come in just for coffee or a beverage, and then there is another section where you can grab a simple sandwich or pizza. The last time we were there, they did not sell alcohol, so if the group was looking for a beer and pizza after the game, another place might be more to the customers' liking. I do not know if the non-alcohol establishment is by choice or has not applied for a license. It has a lot of charm, with lanterns and brick walls that blend with the college's architecture."

"Oh, I like all that you have described. I don't know how you found an ace on your first day here, Charley, but that sounds like a winner."

Charley grinned but kept looking at the sunset. He later added, "I do not stop for tea or coffee, often in a place like that when I am alone. However, today that seemed like the best of my options. It was a central location for some of my stops today. By the way, I have rented a small office that was a converted storefront near that corner today. It will give me a place to work and keep me out of your hair."

"Charley, do you desire to do that?"

"Yes, I do, Ali. It is just a short-term arrangement, and I think it is a win for everyone for the next couple of months. I have agreed to do some handyperson things if they pay for the materials, and in return, I get the space to use for a minimal amount. I wanted a separate working office for a brief time until we feel how this was supposed to fit. We need to transition into this life. I am a bit of a bear outside of my hibernating cave."

"I, for one, believe you will work it out perfectly," said CeCe.

Michael added. "I will work at the home office for the next few days. But let me know if you need anything. Next week I will be gone the whole week. I might have some office furniture in storage at our place. I will take some pictures and send you an email. That way, you can let me know what I can pile in the truck and bring it up to your rental."

"Not that truck we used to move the Christmas tree

from the woods! I remember thinking I should write a eulogy for it when we made it back that afternoon."

"You sound a little like CeCe's dad now, which means we will have to limit your exposure to the darker side of the family tree," Michael kidded.

CeCe gave Michael a hit on the upper arm. "We are just colorful, Michael. My family loves life. It's just that sometimes their life is brighter than others, that's all."

Michael kissed his wife on the cheek. "I like them just the way they are."

"That's better; otherwise, I might have to throw you a pillow, and you can find some comfortable space on the back porch tonight." CeCe gave Michael a big smile and then grabbed his hand. "Come on, partner, let's head home and leave Ali and Charley some time together alone."

Michael responded to the group. "We don't have fights. What we have are discussions that I always seem to lose. I can't find out how she does it, but it seems to turn out that way."

CeCe pulled on his arm to head toward the gate. "I'm not a fighter, but I can be persuasive."

"Yes, that's the part I like," Michael laughed.

After a few hours had passed and the lights were out, Ali touched her husband's jaw in the bedroom's darkness, feeling his whiskers' roughness along his jawbone. "You had a busy day today, Charley," she whispered.

"Mumm," Charley murmured.

"I think you have another life, Charley, that you haven't shared."

Charley grabbed her hand and laid it on his chest. "I foresee now that I must share secrets from my heart, Ali, just not in one day. The last several months have exposed an incredible amount of vulnerability to the chambers of my heart. I should like to spend this night allowing my jiggling mass of muscle in my chest to rest in your arms and sleep soundly as a baby."

"When you put it that way. I shall not say another word and let you enjoy sweet sleep. Snore as you may, I will not jab you in the ribs," remarked Ali. And so, the evening provided sweet dreams for both through the night.

The following day came, and a new day of activities began at the inn on the hill. Charley had been up early before any of the employees had arrived. Filling up his coffee holder with the morning's fresh brew, he snuck into the barn and sat on his makeshift chair with a single light source from an old fixture hanging down from a beam. Charley took out his pad and the little black book and began to read and make notes. At one point, he almost thought he heard rushing water as if it lapped against a pier. He laughed, imaging the echo of the water coming closer to him and then ebbing out as the tide retreated. At that moment, there was a more profound loneliness than Charley could describe. The emotions rested in the soul's chamber that reached out to a lover that he could not see or touch but had felt deeper than any human experience.

Charley found Beaux and his sibling Bea lounging on the private porch on his way back from the barn, barely opening an eye as Charley made it through the door. After changing his clothing and responding to a few emails, Charley was ready to make his first appointment of the day. Ali shared that her time was being taken up with working on a deadline on an article submitted for a magazine. Charley knew she would be active in her office, so he snuck out the private entrance to his truck that he had towed behind the RV from Savannah.

Charley looked at the address from the email he had received. It appeared easy to find. The home was in a cluster of dwellings along a ridge paralleling the interstate. Charley was directed to go to a specific home in the middle of the group of houses along a winding lane. He approached the front door but wondered if he should have used the side door, as the entrance door is not the front door in many of these home styles. However, a middle-aged man came within a few minutes and warmly greeted Charley at the door.

"Reverend Howard?" the man questioned in a friendly tone.

"Yes, good morning. I am Charles Howard. I came to call on Dr. Collins."

"You found me, Reverend Howard. I am glad to welcome you to my home. My wife is out this morning and will be back shortly. She does not like to leave me alone now, but I purposely sent her to the neighbors to do an errand so we could talk. I promised her we would sit on the back porch so she could watch to make sure I was okay from a distance. You know how women are. They stick to you like glue sometimes when all you want is to be alone. Please come on in, and we will go back to the screened-in porch. The breeze should feel good there today. I just made a fresh pot of coffee, but I can get you something else if you prefer some iced tea or a soda."

"I'm fine. I consumed my daily ration of coffee today already. I met your son yesterday, and we can talk about that while I'm here, but I would like to start by talking about you," Charley responded to the ailing pastor. "You must be going through a lot of things right now. I would much rather be here to see if I can assist you somehow."

"Thank you. I appreciate that. That is the main reasons I wanted to meet with you today—just you and me. Yes, the bus ran me over with this diagnosis. It makes one want to put priorities in proper order. The clock is ticking. It clicks for all of us. When the alarm goes off, there will be no more time to take an extra five minutes. When the time is up, that's final." Charley quietly sat in his chair, listening intently. Eventually, Charley graciously moved the conversation to the church. "Why did you ask me to assist with filling in for you, Reverend Collins? I barely came to the area and did not have my mind on being a pastor here. Charley paused for a few seconds. Or perhaps there was another reason to talk to me? I am seldom asked to provide services for those I don't know. How could you trust what I might say?"

"Well, let me start by saying I don't think you are just Charles Howard. You may have ruffled a few feathers in your day and wear war wounds because of it, but I suspect you're too good at what you do to walk away from it all. I heard your sermons on your podcast before I made the request. They spoke to me in personal areas as I've been lying low and have time to think about some things. As for your new marriage, I congratulate you. Ali is a wonderful person, so I asked to talk to you today. I've been holding a secret for a few years now, but I'm bound to tell the truth. My revelation is that Ali is my half-sister. We share the same father."

Charley took a breath in and processed the revelation for a moment. "Does she know this?"

"No, I do not believe Ali ever knew who her father was, and I don't know what she heard growing up. When my father passed away, he told me the information I am sharing with you today. I did not know what to do with the information for some time. I felt God would give me direction. He has the perfect plan. Neither my father nor I want to bring any pain to anyone. I want to do what's right, yet respect my father's intent. Has Ali told you much about her family?"

Charles nodded back negatively. "I know her grandparents raised her. She says nothing but wonderful things about them."

Reverend Collins said, "My father and Ali's mother were both in the service when they were young adults. I am sure my father was young and hot-headed, like most young men his age. He was also married to my mother. He and Ali's mother were an item when they were based overseas somewhere. She eventually became pregnant. Ali's mother returned home with an early dismissal from the military. Soon after Ali was born, her mother died in an auto accident. Her car ran over some ice on the interstate and hit a median cement wall. No one else was involved. Ali's grandparents stepped in, became Ali's legal guardians, and raised her. Evie and James were genuinely kind people. James worked in the steel mill along the river. When he got older, he left for the school district, probably better for his health. Mr. Taylor worked for the school district as a janitor until he was seventy. Evie was a schoolteacher. Pretty much everyone who went to school at that school knew Mrs. Taylor and her husband, James. I went to a different elementary school in the district, but I knew of them. They would have wagon rides at their farm for the schoolchildren in the fall. It was a traditional school field trip for a long time. Whatever love is, Evie and James flowed with it. I know they raised Ali to be a perfect lady. They would have raised her up with God's principals and love."

"Did your father ever meet Ali?" Charley asked.

"As far as I know, Ali never knew him as her father. I know there was an arrangement with her grandparents to provide financial support when Ali went to college. I believe it was anonymously through Dad's attorney. I know this as part of managing my father's estate when he died. The transactions took place so that there would never be in question the purpose and transfer of the funds from certain accounts with my father's authorization. I know that after she bought the inn, he stopped once as a customer. As he recalled, she looked just like her mother, beautiful. My dad was in his late seventies then. His mind was sound, his body destroyed by cirrhosis and cancer. My impression was that he thought highly of Ali's mother. My father was not a pastor like my son and me. He made his money in mining equipment sales after he left the service. He was a man with his quirks, like everyone else. Charles, I most likely won't be around much longer. I look good today, but I know the diagnosis and its typical course. I won't be able to return to preaching. I also know that your home may not be here, given what I heard from your colleagues in Savannah, who want you back desperately. I have been told that you are a man on his journey. You will take a path when others take another road. How you handle the information I told you today is up to you.

I wish only the best for you and your wife. I think the information would be more comforting for her to hear it from you than from me, a stranger."

Charley responded, "You have shared something that your father must have carried a long time. I think he probably wanted to make things right. Your respect for my wife's feelings shows that you, too, want to bring it to closure with peace, and I believe she will accept it that way."

Reverend Collins clasped Charley's hand and whispered, "Thank you, Charles."

Charley soaked in all that he heard. He thanked Reverend Collins for telling him the details of Ali's father. Charley also shared some comforting words before departing. He also requested that his son be recommended to lead the Sunday services. Charley felt this was the best way to move forward with the next generation. I believe you have two sons. What about the other son?"

"My other son is lost, Charles. He has not spoken to me since, well, since I threw him out of the house after he hit his mother while he was trying to take a swing at me."

'Sounds like there's a lot that has happened between you and your son," replied Charley.

"My sons are complete opposites of one another. The one you met yesterday was always easy to raise.

He never caused his mother or me a bit of grief. My other son came out fighting the world since he came into the world. My wife and I tried to work with him."

"One of those little tikes that spewed out lava when he couldn't get his way?" Charley said with a comforting smile.

"You wouldn't believe the battles we've had over simple things. No, you cannot wear your Christmas pajamas to church. No, we can't fill up the ice chest with water and bring the baby alligator home." So Reverend Collins said with a man of lingering frustration.

"That's a lot of pressure being a good father when you're up against a 6-year warrior who's fearless. He most likely challenges you in every way and then adds more to the blindsided challenges."

"I guess you've seen it all in a church your size." Reverend Collins said.

"No, not really. I just hung out on the sidewalk with many of my friends growing up," Charley said. "It gets complicated when they're in their twenties and thirties, and they still challenge authority and boundaries in the world out there. The stuff can be pretty intense."

"Yes." Reverend Collins sighed.

Charley began, "There are good things about children with strong-willed personalities. They have a strong passion for things they believe. They can stand up when others fold because they are not easily motivated by what others think. They usually like to have a choice rather than being told what to do."

"That describes my youngest son pretty well,"

"I think many sons and daughters out there want to be understood by somebody. Being lost does not mean forever. He can still hear your voice. He might have a little electric guitar blasting in his ear right now. Children grow up and make their own choices, but we still hold out a candle just in case they turn toward home."

"Charles, you've been a refreshment for me today. Here I thought I was going to share something important. Instead, you brought something dear to my heart," Reverend Collins said.

As if by magic, Mrs. Collins arrived. Perhaps on instinct or by intensive watching from the neighbor's home, she sensed the time was near to return to the nest to care for her fragile husband. Charley made his way down the sidewalk and shared some pleasantries with Mrs. Collins before tucking himself back behind the wheel of his vehicle. Charley drove down the highway with his sunglasses on, shading his thoughts and feelings from those he passed. Finally, feeling the need, Charley pulled into a parking lot of an establishment selling fresh produce and unique food items. It looked like an interesting place he would like to explore this week. But for the moment, he wanted to cast his thoughts upward.

I do not want to be that foolish again. Tell me what you want. Charley wrote some notes in a pocket notepad. He turned the key over and drove out of the lot.

Charley made several stops before pulling onto the street to park near his rented space. He was happy to see some of the requested supplies arrive. Charley wasn't going to begin any of the hard labor today. He made some measurements, put up a few blinds that had arrived, and took an inventory of outlets and ports he could use. Charley called the local college's art department and saw if some students would like to showcase their artwork in the main room. Hopefully, someone would offer some pieces that were not body nudes; otherwise, he would have some explaining to do not just with church people but also with Ali, who he did not think would appreciate it much. Her opinion mattered to Charley. He worked on the space for the next five hours to make it functional for at least his purposes. He could use his hot spot for now, and the cable internet would be up and ready in a couple of days. He corresponded with those who had sent emails and followed up with other priority issues on his list. He knew Ali would plan dinner at around 6 o'clock, and he would finish up to be home by then. He texted her halfway through installing some shelving and asked if he could make dinner tonight for a change. The specialty grocer on the way home would have what Charley would need. The idea made him feel like his bachelor days when he grabbed what he wanted, went home, and fixed something on the spot. No planning, just doing. It takes adjusting to realize what I'm doing now needs to mash with someone else's doing, Charley thought. With fingers crossed, he hoped that Ali and he could blend into their souls and minds. They both had been single for so long. Charley felt he did not have a road map for what was next, only that he wanted to share this life with Ali for however long they had on this earth. He made a few phone calls and ended his day at the office. The office now included one folding chair, a countertop, one working light bulb, two front window blinds, and four shelves in the niche on the wall behind the countertop. Charley loaded up his gear and looked forward to being home with his growing family of a wife, two dogs, and a cat, all living on the same premises. Thank goodness Ralph, the cat, knew his place in the barn.

After thirty minutes of driving down a two-lane highway, Charley returned to the village where he and Ali lived. He grabbed his grocery bag and headed into the living compartments at the inn. A quick, hot shower turned him into an invigorated man. Charley rolled up his sleeves and went to work.

By the time Ali popped in the side door, the aroma was coming from the oven. The two canines had already been fed and were romping around the great room. After greeting Charley, she snuck a peek in the oven, then smiled back at him with delight. Before she could take her words back, she exclaimed, "Where have you been all my life?" Then she looked as if she showed a sad face. "I am sorry. I am thankful you are here right now and can make a shepherd's pie smell that good! I will pour myself a glass of mineral water and drool right here until it is ready to come out of the oven. Can I do anything?"

"You can take this bowl and start fixing the salad. Do you want another plate or a small bowl?" Charley asked.

"I'm going to need one of those small white plates over there," Ali responded.

Charley took two and gave them to Ali to fill up with greens. He pulled out the pie, cut it into servings, and placed the baking dish on the stove. Ali took her spot on a barstool. She served the meal on porcelain plates, her goblet filled with sparkling water and Charley's with ginger ale.

After dinner was over, Ali spoke up. "I have to finish some revisions, but it shouldn't take me much longer, and I can do it on the patio if you want to lounge in here and relax," Ali said as she got up to stretch her back. She grabbed her laptop before he could answer and took the side door to the porch.

Charley sat and lingered for a moment and rewound the vision in his mind of Ali taking the first sip of her bubbling beverage while laughing at the story she was telling. A tiny drop had splattered onto her white blouse from her goblet. She had carefully dabbed the spot to dry it. He had caught the look of pink nail polish on her manicured fingernails. Something so mundane as that thought lingered in his mind long after she left the room. Charley went to the barn after dinner with two tails wagging on either side of his stride. He finished packing a box for the scheduled pickup tomorrow. He was happy to have completed the set before the end of the month when he promised to ship the order. So many things had transpired after this commission had come in. Luckily, he had it almost completed with his stops on the way up from Georgia. He would have to tell Ali soon, but the list of things he needed to say kept growing longer.

The next day, Charley followed his routine. After taking care of his shipment, he went to his makeshift office. After a couple of hours, he dropped what he was doing and walked up to the local deli. A local direct-ed him to the college bookstore, the closest place in walking distance to pick up an ink cartridge. Michael dropped several boxes of valuable items last night at the inn, and Charley was eager to set some things up today. By the time he returned, he had met quite a few interesting new people. Someone had left him a card on the door while Charley was out. Noteworthy, he was not ready to stop what he was doing and follow up when his head was swimming with must-do items before he left for the day. As he folded up the ladder he had borrowed from the items stored in the barn at Ali's place, the back doorbell rang. *Wondering who that could be?* He found a safe place for the ladder, hurried to the back room, and opened the door. A local delivery person presented him with a package.

"Please sign right here for me," the young woman said and hurried back to her white delivery van.

Charley looked at the address and took the box inside. He cut through the shipping tape and unwrapped the paper around three elegantly cut metal numbers. There was a note inside from the property owner. It read. I took down the numbers after the last tenant was gone. I thought the place looked a bit run down and didn't want it to be identified. I thought you might like to put them back up again, signed by C. Pratt.

Charley took the numbers out of the package and said, "I think I will." Within another ten minutes, the storefront had a street number again posted above the front entrance. Charley picked up his tools and began looking up. Before reaching for the deadbolt, a man walked up to the door. Apprehensively, Charley opened the door.

"Hello there, you must be Charles Howard?" The man said as he put his hand out. He was a grown-up about Michael's age. He was well dressed, and his car out front hinted at that he must be a man of some means.

Charley put out his hand to shake the other man's hand with a questioning expression.

"I am Walter Collins; I left my card earlier. I wanted to know if you ended up buying this place. It looks like you're cleaning up the old office space!"

"No, I'm just short-term leasing space," Charley responded to the stranger. "It just happened that I could do some things for the property owner to give it a fresh look. How can I help you?"

"I wanted to buy a portion of the block up from the corner a few years ago and develop the area. Unfortunately, the deal didn't go through, but it still could be made into something."

"Yes, I think it could. I was just about ready to close up for the day." Charley asked.

"Don't let me hold you back. I just wanted to meet you, thinking you might be the property's new owner. It looks good at what you have done so far. I do not think Mr. Pratt would have done much with it. He likes to hold on to his money tightly."

"I wouldn't know. This space met my need for now, and I appreciated the owner's effort to work with me." Charley replied.

"By the way, what do you do?"

Charley responded. "I have several hats. Today I am a carpenter. On other days, I have been known as a Reverend. I'm new to the area and wanted a space to work."

"For most folks, it's the other way around. You don't give me an impression of being a man of the church?"

"So, what impression would that leave on you?" Charley asked.

"I'm talking about stereotypes, but I think of a Reverend as a self-righteous, controlling, powerless man. I doubt you are the latter if you negotiated with Mr. Pratt for this place?"

"Do you still have interest in developing the street?" Charley asked. He gave no hint of the impression Mr. Collins was making on him. Charley knew the real Mr. Collins was not on the surface.

"You know, I don't know. I am an attorney, as my card says. From time to time, I do work with developers. Today, I stopped by because I saw the change going on in the street. I have barely seen positive changes over the last ten years. Except for the coffee shop a few streets over, it has been a dead community for several years."

Charley probed more. "It sounds like you grew up in the area. What was it like growing up here?"

"It was okay. My father knew everybody in town, so everybody knew the pastor's kids. I guess I hated living under all that attention. It was constraining to me. My best times were when I went off to college and I was my person. I met my first wife there. She made us move back here so she could be close to her parents. That's when I started working on the deal for the property here. I was planning to put professional offices here. The courthouse is up the street and would be a perfect location for attorney's offices. My first wife and I eventually divorced, and I stopped the deal before it got too far along."

"Maybe there's something still here that pulls on your heart. I think you should explore that." Charley responded.

"I don't know. I think I have lost the vision now."

"Well, keep stopping in and check out the changes. Maybe something will inspire you. I bet you have a lot to offer the community," Charley replied.

"I hadn't looked at it that way in a long time. I want to come back and see what you have done in a couple of weeks. Do you preach at any of the local churches now?"

"Not now. I haven't decided what to do since I moved here from Savannah. I'm kind of on a sabbatical, you might say."

"Perhaps I could get you to speak at one of my professional groups in town. I think you would bring something exciting up for discussion."

"We'll see. I want to close for the evening now so I can go home for dinner. I enjoy evenings at home with my wife and tasty food. Pot roast is on the menu on Wednesday, so I hope they kept a plate for me." Charley laughed.

"Thank you, Reverend Howard. I hope we get to

meet again soon." Mr. Collins then turned to walk up the sidewalk, where he parked his car and drove off.

Charley locked up and walked down the street to climb into his truck. He suspected that Mr. Collins carried some scars. He wasn't sure he could help. Charley used his heart to discern the comings and goings of Mr. Collins. He popped in some of his favorite music and began the drive back to the inn.

Twenty minutes later, he was in the parking area at the inn. As he entered the door, he could smell the pot roast. He loved the way Ali spoiled him. Beaux and Bea were the first to come around the corner and hurdled themselves at him to greet him. However, Ali was nowhere in the living quarters. This was strange, thought Charley. Just the kids and me tonight? Charley grabbed a treat to throw at each of the puppies. Then he took them out to the porch. After waiting several minutes for a sign of Ali returning, Charley became concerned. He left the two puppies in the great room while he walked outside and to the service entrance of the inn. The moment he walked in, he felt the stares and the silence. The kitchen manager broke out in tears and left the hallway.

Charley's eyes looked intensely around the room and immediately asked, "Where's my wife?"

One of the staff had the courage to speak up. "I am sorry, sir, your wife took a call earlier from your daughter-in-law. She told us to close after dinner tonight, and then she left for your son's home about an hour ago."

Charley flew out the back door, grabbed his keys, and ran to his car. Was there something wrong with CeCe? Maybe she had been pregnant and miscarried. Of course, she would call Ali for help with something like that. Charley thought CeCe's mother, being in Louisiana, would be too far away to provide emotional support. Ali would be the first-person CeCe would call. We can be there for them. Parents do that for their children. That must be it, Charley kept thinking in his mind. As he pulled into the drive, he spotted Ali's car in the driveway. Charley pulled into the driveway and walked to the front door. When Charley turned the knob, the door was open, so he went on in. Charley could hear Ali's voice muffled in one of the back rooms. He followed the sound. Ali dropped the phone when Charley made it to the archway of one of the spare rooms.

"Oh, Charley," Ali broke down in tears and was so caught up in her emotions that she could not speak further.

"Ali, what's wrong, sweetheart? I am here. Tell me, what has happened?" Charley pleaded as he wiped her tears away. But the tears continued to flow.

"Is CeCe here?" Charley asked. Ali shook her head, meaning "yes".

Charley didn't want to play the interrogator at this

point. "Does Michael know something has happened?"

Ali hyperventilated between sobs. Attempting to calm Ali, Charley instructed her to breathe through her nose and purse her lips to blow out. "Ali, please calm down. Just breathe and catch your breath so you can tell me what's wrong."

Ali finally breathed easy enough to speak. "Michael's gone, Charley," she responded between sobs.

Charley stood back for a minute. "What do you mean? Is he missing? Is he lost? What?" Charley's face went pale with an incredulous expression.

"There was a car accident. He died at the scene. He never made it to the hospital alive." Ali continued to sob continuously. "The officer was here when CeCe called me." Then, with a dazed look, Ali cried, "CeCe's parents are still on the line! I was talking with them."

Charley reached for the phone, but the line was dead. "I will call them back. Where is CeCe?"

"She's in their bedroom. I was trying to come out here to speak privately with her parents." Ali responded.

"What do you know, Ali?" Charley asked, trying to soothe Ali and keep her calm while she was living a nightmare. "I will call CeCe's parents back."

Once Ali shared what she knew, she went back to check on CeCe. He went and checked on CeCe himself before calling CeCe's parents himself. Ali sat near the bottom of the bed. Charley put his arms around CeCe as he would a daughter of his own and said some soothing words. She stopped sobbing for a moment and nodded her head in affirmation. Then, Charley left the room to reach out to the Robichaud family.

Richard was the one who answered and told Charley that they had picked up the first bit of news from CeCe before she had dropped the phone in hysterics. Richard had already made flight arrangements for himself and his wife and would arrive later in the evening. Richard was unsure of what had happened when he got the call as CeCe could barely get a sensible word out without crying. However, he knew something heart-wrenching had happened, and CeCe needed them. Steven supposedly received a message at a worksite from someone in the company. "I had to tell him what I knew when he called here. We are just about ready to leave to catch our plane," Richard said, and asked Charley if he could speak to his daughter. Charley walked back to the room where CeCe sat, eyes red from crying, hugging a sweatshirt that Michael wore when he went out to run.

"CeCe, this is your father," Charley said as he held the phone to her.

Richard could hear her sobs through the phone. "CeCe, honey, your mother and I will be there in just a few hours. Please don't do anything until we get there. Your mother and I love you. You are still our baby girl; we will be there for as long as you need us!"

"Okay, Daddy," CeCe muffled down her sob. CeCe returned the phone to Charley, gesturing that she did not want to talk anymore.

More information became available once the Robichauds arrived. Another employee was driving Michael to a worksite only a few miles from the office. The other gentleman's injuries were not life-threatening. However, Michael's side of the vehicle took the brunt of the hit when a truck in the next lane attempted to avoid a car entering from an entrance lane and moved too far to the left. That spun the car that Michael was in around. His side received a direct hit again from the vehicle behind them. The accident occurred while Michael was in a company vehicle. Therefore, human resources needed to be involved. Someone had volunteered to work on the company's end to compile the essential information and documentation that CeCe will need as quickly as possible.

Ali and Charley stayed halfway through the night and eventually returned to the inn once everyone went to some sleep. When they returned the following day, CeCe was sitting with her parents in the dining room. Her tears had stopped, but her eyes were red and swollen. Ali joined them at the table while Charley remained standing, bracing himself against the wall.

CeCe looked up at Charley and asked, holding her tears back and making her request in a deliberately calm tone. "Charley?"

"Yes?"

"Do you think Michael could be buried in Savannah, maybe near your parents?" CeCe asked with tears pooling in her eyes again.

Charley was taken aback for a moment at CeCe's request. However, he knew the answer to the question immediately. "Yes, CeCe. There's a plot that is owned and is on the backside of my parent's headstone. Michael can rest with my parents."

"Thank you. Michael would like that." Then CeCe broke down, causing all the others to sob at the table freely.

"I will make the call," Charley said, tears streaming silently down his cheeks. Charley was unsure of the reason for the choice, but he would respect CeCe's decision.

"Thank you," CeCe responded as she gathered her composure. "I would like a service here for his friends and the company associates and then fly the coffin down to Savannah for a private service the next day at the gravesite with family. Do you think we can arrange that?"

"I will take care of it," Charley said while holding his composure.

CeCe nodded to show she agreed with the plan, holding back her sobs.

Chapter 9

IT HAD BEEN TWO days since the funeral. Ali flew back the day after with CeCe and her parents. Charley stayed behind and promised that he would return in a week. Although Charley could provide several explanations, the actual reason was that he did not want to leave. Charley wrestled with his thoughts. Wouldn't Ali feel the same? I'm not a tower of strength like everyone would like me to be. He looked up at his friend, who now was causing an impediment to Charley's self-pity party. "I was told my great-grandfather was a horse thief who never had a penny that was his own all his life. He died from gangrene that set in after receiving a gunshot wound to the leg while climbing out of a window of a home that wasn't his own, with a female that wasn't family, most likely doing something that we don't mention at Sunday dinner. Supposedly, he had a message from God on his deathbed and confessed his faith. How is this man allowed to be with my son now?

Michael had a beautiful soul, adored and generous to a fault, like knowing an angel. I'm not worthy of being here with all my flaws. He should be here, not me."

"Charley, I hope I came in time. You don't have to become a funny drunk," Bob said as he brewed some coffee. He looked at the long-necked bottle still in a gift box sitting on the counter. "You're lucky I found you tonight before you caused damage to yourself." Bob cracked the seal and poured the amber contents into the sink. "Waste of good money going down the drain! But, in your case, it's the right thing to do," Bob said sarcastically. Then, with good intentions, he pitched the bottle into the trash. "Do you have any more?"

Charley pointed to the cabinet on the left. "Remind me to thank you later," said Charley, with his head down.

"Hey, this is what genuine friends are like." Bob opened the cabinet, looked at the label, and held on to the bottle he found. "Ali is worried about you and calls me every day to check on you. She needs you, man, but she needs you in one piece, not like this."

"I want to come back here, Bob, to live. Savannah is my home." Charley continued with his lament. "Michael is buried here. I don't want to leave him here alone," mumbled Charley.

Bob pulled two mugs out of the cabinet and filled both with coffee before sitting across from Charley. "Then let Ali know how you feel. You both have been through a very traumatic loss. It's tough, but you will have to shove your two legs under you again. You and I both know Michael's memory is honored where those who love him remember him here," Bob responded as he touched Charley's heart. "I don't need to tell you that because you believe that more than I do. It's the pain coming out of your mouth and holding you back from comforting Ali right now. Ask her if she would consider coming back to Savanah! Carole and I want you back, but we don't matter. It's what is the right choice for you and Ali."

"She wanted me to be her warrior, and I'm failing miserably," Charley said with a sad look.

"We all have times when we don't look like heroes. That is why there is the word jerk in English," responded Bob.

"If we keep this conversation going in this direction, I'm going to need a drink," Charley said while rubbing his eyes.

"No, you're not. Knock me out cold if you think I'm going to let you do that. You are going to walk through this fire. Remember, four men were in that fiery furnace in one of those chapters of the book that you so love to read. He is in this one with you, too. You will drink some of this black coffee, and then you will clean yourself up. After passing my inspection, you will call your lovely wife and tell her you are alive. After that, I suggest you get on your boney knees and thank the one above that he has given you a guardian angel who has put up with you this long. I'm doing this because I love your brother. Now get in there and take a shower. You look a bit rumpled to me, if you get my drift. I will check on you in an hour. Don't bolt the door because I know how to break into your house!"

"Yeah, yeah. Wait a minute. I thought you didn't read the black book. How do you know about the story of Daniel in the lion's den?" asked Charley as he waved his friend away. He took two sips of the coffee and made a face.

"I know stories, Okay!" Bob responded with his sarcastic wit. "My mother was a protestant. I will confess that the stained glass windows drew her to the church we attended when I was a child. The services, as I recall, were humorless and dry in content."

"Remind me to send you a couple of dry sermons of my own for being a pesky neighbor!" Charley taunted. "Ouch!" Charley yelped as he hit his foot on the leg of the kitchen table, attempting to get up. "Has anyone said you are a pain in the neck?" Charley growled out as he walked past Bob to the hallway.

"Not in the last thirty-eight minutes, but you mentioned that in the earlier part of this conversation about an hour ago." Once Bob heard the water running, he left out through the back door carrying the bottle of alcohol that Bob had pillaged from Charley's cabinet.

"So, how is he?" Carole asked when her husband

would make it back to the house.

"Pretty rough. He's hurting everywhere. He just buried a son. His marriage does not have old deep roots, so that is not grounding him now. His relationship with Ali must have been complicated, given that whatever separated them kept Ali and Charley apart for almost thirty years. I am not sure what ghosts are haunting him the most. He said he wanted to come back here to live, so he is struggling with that. I want to help. But Charley must push through this painful time. Charley has always been a solid guy. I'm almost glad Ali isn't here to see him like this." Bob said. "I have faith in Charley. He will find how to bring the shattered pieces together. But that doesn't mean scars disappear after they heal. Sometimes those scars are our monuments in life. They leave us with a mark that stays with us like a learned lesson." said Bob, looking at the clock.

"From a female's viewpoint, I think Ali would want to be with him so they could support each other right now. I think it's a very vulnerable time for them both," Carole added to the discussion.

Bob sat back in his chair and picked up a book while allowing time to pass. Thirty minutes later, Bob quietly walked back over through the hedges. He could briefly hear Charley's voice on the phone as he cracked open the kitchen door. He could tell from the conversation that Charley was talking with Ali. Let them have their time together, Bob decided.

In the morning, Charley was packing the car when Bob was ready to leave for work. Bob stopped in front of the driver and rolled down the window. "It looks like you're heading on out. I think you are going back to Pennsylvania."

"Yes, Ali and I talked a long-time last night. I left you a note tied to your doorknob. Thanks, Bob!" Charley said somberly.

"Anytime, brother. Call or text when you get there so Mrs. won't worry and I won't have to arrange a search party. Okay?"

"I will," Charley responded. He waited until Bob turned at the end of the street before he went back to loading up the car. It would be a long day, not only physically, but mentally. He felt tormented by the memories of following the hearse from the airport, knowing that Michael's body lay within. He showed robust strength while holding Ali up when she almost collapsed as they lowered their son's body to the ground. He tried to shake off the memories, but he was still bleeding from a wound that people could not see. Charley almost lost his way again last night, using his old pattern to cope with pain. He has more power and strength than his recent behavior reflected."

Chapter 10

IT WAS AROUND EIGHT at night when Charley pulled into the inn. He pulled out his duffle bag that had the necessities and entered the private entrance. Ali was on the sofa where she had fallen asleep. Beaux and Bea had curled up on the floor beside her. He returned his things to the bedroom and took the dogs outside for a few minutes.

When he came back in, Ali was still sleeping on the sofa and had not moved. Charley didn't want to wake her, so he went to the kitchen to make some coffee and stretched out in the recliner. Then, just after midnight, she stirred. "Hello, gorgeous!" Charley whispered.

Ali stretched out her legs and tried to get a sense of where she was. She smiled, moved to the recliner, and sat on the ottoman close enough to reach out to her husband. "I missed you, Charley. I was also concerned

"Well, he's at the little office he's been working on, but he's available. I'm sure he will help. What is it?"

"I have something to give Charley. It was at Michael's desk as we packed up his things in the office in the barn. I think Michael would want you to know about it, too." CeCe stopped for a moment to control her sobs. "I need to give this to Charley."

Ali's voice was gentle. "Of course, CeCe. Do we need to come now?"

CeCe responded, "I have it with me. Whenever you can be here would be fine."

"I am calling Charley right now. I will text you when he says he can get there, and I will meet him there. Is there anything else we can bring or do for you, CeCe?"

"No, Dad and Mom are still here, and the company is arranging for a move coming to take the few things that I want to take with me to Louisiana. We're just trying to clear the house of what I want to keep before leaving with my parents. I don't want to be around when people are coming to move things from the house."

"Charley texted me back and said he could be there in thirty minutes. How does that sound?" Ali asked.

"That's fine," CeCe responded. "I will see you both, then."

Ali stopped what she was doing and left the inn in

the manager's hands. Ali had left Rona and Richard to help CeCe since they had all returned from the funeral. She tried to give them some space as it seemed like she only reminded CeCe of Michael. It was hard to stay away, but she tried to do what was best. Rona and Richard called several times to ask or share something as they went through some personal items. Finally, Ali found her keys and headed out to her car, thinking that CeCe must have discovered something of Michael's that would be meaningful to Ali and Charley. She drove to Michael and CeCe's home and anxiously waited for Charley to arrive. Ali thought of those months that CeCe and Michael spent remodeling the home Ali's parents had left for her. Michael had loved the spectacular views of rolling hills and distant dairy farms that dotted the vista to the east and west. The woods provided privacy and protection for the deer that grazed across the grassy pastures.

Charley pulled into the drive a few minutes behind Ali. He walked to her door to open it and took her hand as they walked together to the front door. Charley rang the doorbell and stepped in when Rona came to the door.

"It's good to see both of you," said Rona and hugged Charley and Ali. Charley saw the boxes piled in the entryway. Rona explained that the truck would arrive tomorrow to move the things that CeCe wanted to keep. She added, "CeCe is going to let many large pieces stay in the house. But she wants to keep some things, so we're trying to keep those things separate. CeCe and Richard just came up from the barn to take a break and sit on the back porch. Let's go out there, and I'll get you something to drink. Would you like a soda or bottled water?"

Ali answered, "I'm fine."

"Me too," Charley said. They both followed Rona to the screened-in porch.

"Well, Charley and Ali, that was quick. It's good to see you both." Richard replied.

"We just stopped for a break, so it is perfect timing. CeCe, I think your mother and I will go out a little. We probably need to do a few errands, like pick up some light bulbs and door stripping tape that I told you I would fix. Michael's little darlings in the barn used the old stripping as teething toys. It won't take me a few minutes to put a new strip up. Give us an hour to pick up some things at the hardware."

"Okay, Dad. See you in a little while. Love you!" CeCe said.

"Your mother used to say that. Now she just says 'bye'." Her father smiled back.

"Come on, you old toot," Rona smiled at her husband and grabbed his arm to guide him to the door. "Bye." She waved back.

"You see!" Richard looked back and waved to

those remaining.

CeCe went to the table and picked up an envelope that was on the table. "Charley, I have something for you. Michael promised he would not reveal the contents of this envelope, thinking that he would outlive his grandparents and you. He thought the secret would end with him. He was trying to respect someone's wishes. However, I am not Michael, so I do not feel the same fidelity. I also think the truth has more healing than secrets. The envelope is for you, Charley," CeCe put the packet in his hands.

Charley looked at the envelope and the return address. "This is from the attorney's firm of my parents," Charley said to Ali as he looked inside and saw a letter and a stub from what appeared to be a check and a deposit slip into an account with Michael's name on it. Charley looked down again and pulled out a white envelope with a letter inside. Charley noted the date from a few years earlier. The envelope also contained two pictures, each falling to the floor face down. Charley read the letter's contents and then handed it to Ali to read for herself. Charley then reached down to pick up the pictures from the floor. One photo was of Charley standing in front of the church. His mother had taken the photo after the wedding of a family friend. The other was an older picture, most likely made from a camera that took photos by pulling on a black tab of paper to get the photo like the one his parents used. It showed a young couple of college-aged standing beside a Christmas tree.

Ali was the first to speak. "She knew about Michael, Charley! All these years, she knew she had a grandson!"

"CeCe, when you and Michael came to church that Sunday morning, did Michael know who I was?" Charley said, with his hands shaking.

CeCe nodded affirmatively. "All that Steven said at the wedding was true. When Steven put the pieces together, he encouraged Michael to meet you. Steven didn't say how it should happen. He just felt that it was the right thing to have you meet. It wasn't Michael's decision to go to Savannah on business trips so much. Michael would have stayed in the northeast office, closer to his mother, or in Louisiana to be with my folks more often. Steven was a factor in attempting to link them. Michael and Steven were really like brothers. If Steven saw something that caused Michael pain, he would try to find some way to resolve the pain. When Michael and I went for the weekend for our anniversary, there was no plan that we would look for or attempt to find you. That weekend we were on our own, doing our own thing. Then, Sunday came. Neither of us wanted to leave when we got up that morning. We were so happy. I saw your church while we were driving by on our way to the hotel when we got there late Saturday afternoon. I didn't know about you, Charley. Michael and I took a walk later that night and when we returned from dinner, I looked at the service times of the church I had remembered earlier in the day. The times stuck in my head. The following day, Michael indulged me by attending services at the church I had seen the day before. I love old churches, and we've done that before when we traveled. He never said a word about the church I had selected. Michael walked up the stairs outside the church where you were standing, shaking people's hands as they entered. There were many people around you, but I remember we were close enough that his hand touched you when we went by. We found a seat somewhere in the middle of the sanctuary. He never said a word while we were in the pew. Michael never let on that he knew who you were while we were in Savannah."

"I remember that day, CeCe. Ali, there was something there that I could feel that day. I can't explain except through what I believe. People would say it was just coincidental. But I don't believe that. Something happened."

CeCe continued. "Michael told me about what had happened in Savannah when we returned a few days later. I was in shock! He then told me what he knew about his biological father. He knew you from the photo that your mother had sent. I didn't read the letter until today, so I know now what he held close to his heart since he received it. He had received it before we were married. It made him so happy to build a father-son relationship with you. Michael took a risk at Christmas. He wasn't sure how it would go, but he also felt that love hadn't died. It worked out as he had hoped. Charley, when you and Ali got married, it made Michael's wish would come true." CeCe tried to remain composed as she went on. "Now, do you see why I chose Savannah as a place for Michael's burial? I think he would have wanted that."

Ali responded, with tears streaming down her face. "His forgiveness is deeper than anything I can conceptualize. He never told me about receiving this letter."

Charley put the things back in the envelope. "Thank you, CeCe," Charley said and hugged her. "My son was married to a beautiful woman. Michael would want you to be happy."

"I believe that too. It's just going to take some time. I kept some photos in a separate box that I thought you might like to keep. I kept most of the wedding pictures, but I had some other ones, like Michael using the sled the first time it snowed heavily here on the property after getting married. So let me get that box, so it doesn't get put in the wrong stack."

"Thank you, CeCe. I will cherish everyone," Ali said.

Richard and Rona returned, bringing in some takeout from one of the little eateries. Well, it's not gourmet, but we can all share a sandwich and a beverage. Charley helped to move a few boxes up from the barn. Ali helped with some things in the house. It was the last thing to be done before tomorrow. CeCe wandered through the rooms touching the door frames and glass as she recalled memories of her and Michael selecting materials for the home. It was all just precious memories now.

Later that evening, Charley and Ali sat quietly in the great room of their home. "You're noticeably quiet, Ali. Do you want to talk?" Charley asked.

"No, not really, but I am thinking about Charley. Do you mind if I sit up for a while alone tonight? I need to handle some things in my heart this evening to find happiness again. Michael was my entire adult life. Charley, I think I want to move back to Savannah. It feels good to me to be there. I could let someone manage this place. I prefer to sell and let go of my life here. It has no more purpose for me now. I will make some calls in the morning."

"I think that is sound reasoning, Ali. I 'm glad to hear that you want to find that joy again. In the morning, you can start filling my head with all those ideas you nurture. I will support you in any way I can."

"Thank you, Charley," Ali responded. Several hours later, she crawled into bed, trying not to wake Charley. Beaux and Bea didn't move an inch from their comfortable niche at the foot of the bed. She whispered to Charley, "We are going to go through this fire, Charley."

Chapter 11

ANOTHER SOMBER WEEK PASSED. Charley and Ali were determined to create a plan to move forward. Charley's professional experience trained him to help those grieving. However, some wounds leave permanent scars no matter how well one tries to recover. Charley was reminded daily of something that would trigger Michael's memory, yet his image was fading. Charley still felt the eagerness of wanting to hear Michael's voice on the speakerphone. For only a brief time, Charley acknowledged Michael as his son. That was the happiest of Charley's days. However, Charley found himself isolated moments during the week when the loss would strike and his emotions were held hostage. Anger would pour into his soul, and he wanted to fight the darkness. Charley didn't like this phase. Was it not for Michael's perfect response to love and forgiveness Charley didn't think he could extinguish his fury?

Michael filled himself with the right things, regardless of how unfair life was. Charley was hungry to fill that ache caused by Michael's death. By Friday, Charley had a plan that he thought would work for everyone. He opened the office space promptly at 9 o'clock. One of the college students came in the morning, and another would rotate in and cover the afternoon. Charley had a list of specific things for them to do. He then walked to the back workroom and put on his goggles. His hands worked the equipment, and the woodblocks formed. He sawed, sanded, and pounded. A shape appeared from the attention each piece received. Charley felt energized as his hands felt the textures. A melody came to his mind, and he felt a sensation on the inside. Charley could not put it into words. It was as if someone was working with him as he continued into the afternoon.

Ali left the inn after lunch. There had been a bridal shower party in the sunroom and a sorority tea luncheon in the private dining room. The other patrons were a mixed group of travelers, couples, and ladies' groups that met for monthly teas. Hazel had things well in control as most groups were breaking up as Ali planned her escape. She checked on Bea and Beaux, who appeared to be quite content. Ali picked up a piece of paper that showed the office address that Charley had rented. She smiled for a moment. After picking up a couple of baked items from the kitchen next door, Ali took off in her car. She drove to the next town in the area. As she got closer to the university, more pedestrians were seen. College life in the summer did not mean no people. It just meant less than usual. One could always find a student who stayed the summer for studies, work, or both. Employees found their way off-campus at various times of the day. The legal crowd remained within the three-block radius of the courthouse. Ali thought the address she had for Charley's rented space was on the fringe of both groups. Ali made a right hand at the next red light. She saw a coffee house just ahead on the left. I bet that is the one CeCe had talked about, Ali thought. She drove until she reached the next intersection. The street marked an area where some of the older buildings stood. She saw the numbers above the door on one storefront that matched Charley's address. A parking space was available just a few car lengths away, and she pulled in. Picking up her purse and the box of treats she brought from the inn, Ali walked to the front. She could see that the entrance had been freshly painted and clean blinds in the front window. She walked into a large, bright room with a couple of benches and paintings on the wall. A young man greeted Ali from behind a partition.

"My name is Bryan. How can I help you?"

"Hello Bryan, I am Ali Howard. Would my husband, Charley, be here?"

"Of course, Mrs. Howard. He is back in the first office on the right, I think. At least, I think he finished in the back room. Go ahead back. I watch the front for a few hours every other Friday."

"Thank you, Bryan." Ali slipped on the back

through a hallway that also smelled of paint.

The door was closed. Ali knocked lightly and opened the door slowly.

Charley was talking to someone on his laptop. His eyes grew wider, and he smiled, waving Ali to come closer. "Tanner, this is my wife. Ali, I will bring her around sometime when we are in Savannah."

"Hi, Tanner!" Ali said through the computer web camera.

"Tanner is one of my colleagues in Savannah," Charley said to Ali. "Tanner, how about I follow up with you on Monday? You can email me more details about what we were talking about over the weekend."

"Sure enough," Tanner responded. "Ali, tell your husband to come around when you are in town. You might help give him a sweater disposition some days."

"Absolutely," Ali replied, and waved back at the screen.

"So, what is it you do, Charley? Am I married to an undercover government agent?" Ali asked with a grin and a wary eye.

"I need to tell you more. I have wanted to. Things seemed to keep coming up. It's not bad or undercover, but I have some things to share with you. Several things have been on my mind that I need to share, and maybe it's about time I told you more things."

"You're scaring me, Charley," Ali responded with a concerned look.

"It's not bad, at least my work with Tanner and the boys, as I call them. How about I show you around? First, what do you have in that box?"

"I brought something we baked this morning at the inn for the children's party."

"I like it already. Can I peek?" asked Charley with a smile.

"I think as long as you've been a good guy all these years."

Charley blew out his breath. "You had to say that. Okay, let me think." He stretched his body to look in the box. "I have an idea. Let's go up to the coffee shop and get something. We can split one of those things that looks like a chocolate saucer with cream, which can only mean one thing. What I need to say will take a while, so let's start with the good stuff first. Let me take you on a walk to the back room." Ali put the box down and followed Charley. "This is what I was working on this week, and I will ship it back to Tanner soon."

"Oh, Charley! The table is what you've been doing here all this time! Finally, it makes sense. You are an artist, Charley!" Ali exclaimed.

"I work with my hands to make things. You saw the chair I made you. This piece is something else I'm making for a shop that I co-own with Tanner and a couple of other men. We all work with our hands to make things. It is therapeutic for us. We share a similar purpose."

"Charley, this is a gift!"

"Yeah, some people might say that, but it's a part of who I am."

"So, you've been hiding out here to work?" Ali asked.

"There are many reasons for space," responded Charley. "I needed a place that was mine to work. It gives me an identity. It's messy work sometimes." Charley looked at his watch. "I think Bryan has packed up for the day. Let's lock up and walk up the street, and I will share some more tales about me." Charley locked up the smaller office he had been in earlier. He grabbed the keys and stuck one of the chocolate, football-like creations that Ali had brought in a small brown bag. "Let's go." They walked up to the coffee shop that Charley had stopped for the first time just a few weeks ago. Ali ordered an iced coffee while Charley ordered his unsweetened tea.

"Let's go out to the patio. It looks like we have the spot to ourselves," Charley responded. Charley broke open the seal from the plastic wrap and split the cake into two pieces. "I am not ashamed of saying some carbohydrates are worth it!" He took a corner of the chocolate gob and chewed it with a smile. "Remind me later to tell you just how good this is. But I must finish what I need to say to you."

"Okay, I'm your captive listener of all the bad things you've done."

"You are making this tough, but you need to know me. What do I like, what don't I like, and what makes me such a hard man to love? Let us start with a simple question. What is my favorite beverage?"

Ali responded, "I guess it is iced tea. You are always drinking iced tea all the time at home or when we go out."

"Wrong," Charley responded with no hesitation. "It's tequila. I will take a whiskey as a strong second. I cannot drink either. The substance in the bottles takes control of me. What do Tanner and the boys have in common? That was a rhetorical question. I don't expect you to answer that question. The answer is the like for the same drink with the same effect. We are men who keep each other from self-destruction. Our mission is to help other men like us."

"Charley, I didn't know," Ali answered softly. "It doesn't change the way I think of you. How long have you been sober?"

"A little over twenty-five years ago. I started drinking hard liquor after you left. It then drew me into the dark side of alcohol. My parents were helpless to fix my problem. Now I know why. That letter my mother sent Michael confirms what I think I knew, at least partly. I bottled many feelings, accepting their decisions on things that affected my life. I could say more, but I don't want to go there right now. I found myself in a pit. I came to an understanding of who God is. Ultimately, I had to choose to stop being self-destructive. I did not do it alone. I was carried through the fire by true friends. It humbles me to this day, and I will never forget their help during that dark time. That is why I went to the seminary. It was my choice, not my parents' choice. The night of Steven's accident, it was not because he was in a car. He was a pedestrian drunk after being in a fight. I saw him on the ground from a distance. I did not see the driver, which occurred on a dark rainy street when the streets were wet in a poorly lit area. I ran to him because I saw an image of me at that age. I wasn't willing to let him die that night because I wanted him to have to lead a full life."

Ali responded, "Charley, the vine connects us all. I think you also heard something that night, too. Perhaps some heard another message that came to your aid. Others may have heard another message entirely, but you heard the message that comforted Steven that night."

"Yeah, I know. Sometimes I need to remember what keeps me alive," Charley said while attempting to contain his composure. "Before I sob like a baby and make a fool of myself, let's walk back to the car," Charley said. Before pushing away from the table, he moved his hand to the cake like dessert. "I'm going to finish another bite of my half. If you have more in that box, you bring them home. I'll call dibs on it tonight with a cold glass of milk."

Ali laughed as she wiped a crumb from his lip. "Then let's get that box and get you home."

Later that night, Ali and Charley were sitting on the floor, splitting their time between attending to Beaux and Bea and separating laundry into his and her piles. Charley held up a skimpy piece of underwear and laughed. "Most definitely yours."

Ali laughed. "Of course, it's mine. It's pink! Your clothes only fall in the hues of black, off black, and blue!" she teased.

"Well yeah. It helps me coordinate my wardrobe and keep my clothing allowance down. It also helps me dress faster in the morning for work. I've got the style down: blue pants, blue socks, white shirt for weekdays. On weekends it's blue or black jeans, a matching tee, and socks. How can you go wrong with that? Leaders in the business world have held on to this idea for some time. They stole it from me." Charley smiled back. Charley wrestled with Beaux over a bone toy and threw it behind the sofa. Beaux tore after it and happily brought it back, laying it by Charley's feet. The pup's owner responded with praise by petting the dog's head.

"Ali, how much do you know of your father?" Charley

asked out of nowhere.

"I don't know anything. Why do you ask?" Ali responded with a bit of shock.

"I know who he was, Ali. I've meant to tell you since the Monday after my arrival here."

"How would you know that? You didn't know anyone here." Ali asked.

Charley responded, "Remember the message you gave me when I arrived in Pennsylvania from Reverend Collins?"

"Yes," Ali responded, thinking back on the message for her husband.

"Reverend Collins lives a few towns over. He is the father's younger son and pastor of a church in the next township. I responded to a request to fill in for a pastor who has had to take a permanent medical leave at a church. They had placed some feelers with the denomination on who might be available. The whole thing was odd, but I followed up with a phone call and then a visit to the church and the ailing pastor as a courtesy. Unfortunately, Reverend Herbert Collins was diagnosed with a terminal illness. As a fellow pastor, I followed up with him the next day to inquire about his health and asked if there was something I could do. The unique thing about this man was that he claimed to be your half-brother, Ali."

Ali sat straight up for a moment with a startled

expression. "The name is not familiar to me. My grandparents never let on that they knew anything about my father. My birth certificate stated my father was unknown."

Charley continued. "Supposedly, your real father and mother met while in the military. He was married. I don't believe his wife or children knew anything about you or your mother's relationship. The older Mr. Collins passed away a few years ago. He made a living selling mining equipment, from my understanding."

"To be crude, I guess I was a bit of trash he didn't mean to bring home?" Ali responded sarcastically.

"I don't think it was like that exactly. I'm not condoning your father since he was already married, but I got the feeling that there was some relationship between him and your mother. Young men and women bond together to create a unit. Stuff happens. I'm sure there's a lot of fear, tension, and loneliness that someone in the military experiences. I can't tell you I have experienced what they have experienced because I've never worn a soldier's boots."

"Do you think he ever tried to see me?" Ali asked.

"I didn't believe so when you were a child. According to his son, he came in as a customer once after you bought the inn. He would have been an older man then. He said that you looked just like your mother," Charley responded. "He had put away some funds for you when you went to college and made some sort of anonymous arrangement with your grandparents or through a third party with your grandparents."

Ali thought for a moment with her eyes looking up. "I remember receiving money from a private scholarship through the church my grandparents attended. I never questioned it because I trusted my grandparents completely. It was a private scholarship from a third party. I did not save the records as that was so many years ago. It wasn't a lot of money, but it covered my books and some fees. Wow!" Ali pondered that idea for a while. "That piece of information does not change things for me. My grandparents were my parents. They gave me love. They were around when I cried when my first boyfriend broke up with me. My grandparents listened to my sobs for being teased by the other kids in the fourth grade for liking turnips as my favorite food instead of pizza or hamburgers like the other kids. My grandmother was a wonderful cook, so maybe she was better at cooking turnips than their mamas." Ali responded with a bit of a laugh and paused for a few minutes. "When I became pregnant, they accepted me back into their home. It must have been like my mother returning home." Ali said, while holding back a sniffle.

Charley tried to lighten the mood by tossing one of the folded socks to Beaux. "What makes you happy, Ali?" Charley asked.

"That's not simple to answer. I wouldn't say I like to do laundry, but I remember loving sorting and folding Michael's little outfits when he was a baby. I enjoy writing my books. I look at life when I write about distinct characters in my stories. It allows me to understand others and reach out to them. We all have pains and challenges. My imagination lets me go there and feel the pain and pleasures of others, which gives me a better understanding of my world."

"I can see that," Charley responded. Then, with a teasing intent, Charley added, "The chocolate fudge cheesecake with raspberry sauce idea for your book cover was brilliant. It sure sent a powerful message to me. My salivary glands were in action before I made it to the table of contents."

"Charley, I wrote that book five years ago. When did you see that book?" Ali asked with surprise.

"I saw it at a bookstore in Savannah when I was browsing for a gift for our secretary at the church who loves to cook. I recognized the author's name."

"That's fascinating! When you came on Christmas Eve, did you know you would see me?" Ali asked.

"It was not on my agenda. I was coming to spend Christmas with Michael and CeCe. That was my only thought. I was so grateful that Michael allowed me in his life that nothing else mattered. Things moved along so fast during the few days I was here. I was soaking in the magic of being a father. CeCe's parents were also there, so my time was also spent enjoying them. I can honestly say that when I saw you in person again after all the years, my breath left my chest. I did not feel empty. I was alive far more than I had been in years."

"Thank you, Charley. That is dear to my heart. I am overwhelmed right now. With feelings." Ali went back to her task of working with the laundry. "No more secrets tonight, Charley. My heart can't take any more today." After a few quiet moments of finishing the stack of socks, Ali looked back up at Charley. "Life with you isn't ordinary, is it?" She leaned over against his shoulder and snuggled closer to him.

"Never ordinary and seldom easy," Charley stated in a matter-of-fact tone and then gave her a wink.

The next few days were a time of adjusting to change. CeCe was now safe with her family several states away. Signatures on documents severed the ties to the fairytale she once lived in and the present she could barely face. The moving truck left for the interstate, carrying the only belongings she was to keep. CeCe would always remain a daughter in the hearts of Ali and Charley, but they knew this was the right decision for her. She needed to move on to the next leg of her journey.

The inn would also soon change ownership, as potential buyers were alerted that the inn that Ali owned and operated was up for sale. It was time for Ali to get used to being a wife to Charley Howard. She was learning more each day. Sentimental reasons saved a few items, but the bulk of things would be donated or sold on the property. It was a busy time for

Ali. Visitors stopped to help and express appreciation for what she had done for their community. Ali thought of the things that meant nothing out of the ordinary. Yet, to someone, she found out how those little things meant a lot. The repair person patched up his marriage over a dozen soft molasses cookies that Ali had sent with him on Christmas Eve. He came to repair a toilet hose that had burst in one of the guest baths late that afternoon. Those cookies were motivation to stop off at his ex-wife's home that night. For the last five years, Joe, the handyperson, has not had to spend Christmas Eve alone. Ali was happy to send his wife the cookie recipe when she heard about how they got back together.

The inn manager reminded Ali of when a rabbit went AWOL for an Easter photoshoot at the inn. We captured the nibbling predator in the salad that was planned as the featured recipe for a magazine article. That was when Ali thought of changing the supper entrée to rabbit a la orange. Luckily, the photographer was a vegetarian and talked her out of her idea. Ali was happy to laugh about it now with Hazel, but it was quite a stress point then. As Ali was organizing her departure, she felt her staff and colleagues expected the change. With her recent marriage and loss of her son, Ali needed a change. It was comforting to leave with warm feelings of friendship and support that she had received in the next chapter of her life.

Charley had a few things on his mind as well before leaving. His list was shorter, but perhaps more challenging to address. Charley let that go in his morning quiet time in the barn. Charley just sat for a few moments today. He was planning to stay around and help Ali with her list of things to be completed. So, after letting the college volunteer go home at noon. Charley had the rental space to himself. He had made phone calls to share his plans to take specific action steps.

Mr. Collins's son, Walter, arrived late in the afternoon, and the two men walked around the work area in the back and grabbed a couple of stools to talk.

"You've done a fine job of making the space workable again. I'm sure the owner will hate seeing you leave." Walter said.

"Well, that may be true, but a new tenant can always replace me. However, recent events have caused my wife and me to re-look at what matters most. We are moving back to where I am from and where we spent time together when we were young." Charley replied. "If I may ask, why did you want to purchase this property a few years back when you had an idea of developing the street?"

"It doesn't matter now," Walter mumbled as he looked down at the floor with a dejected expression. Then, he paused for a few moments and added, "My grandfather on my mother's side had his accounting office here. When I was about 4 or 5, my grandmother would bring me to his office on a Wednesday. That was a day in the week when some businesses closed early. We would walk up to where that new coffee shop was up the street. Customers could sit at the counter or in booths against the wall. I bet you remember the kind."

Charley smiled, "I sure do."

"I loved that time in my life. I loved my grandparents too, at least my mother's parents. They always enjoyed things and people around them." Walter said.

"Sounds like they were pretty happy."

"Yeah, they were happy and seemed to spread their attitude on life wherever they went." Mr. Collins when on to say. "His face would light up when my grandmother came to the office. He was proud of having a grand-son as an attorney. My practice was starting when I thought about this block, so I thought I would do something with the property to make him proud." Mr. Collins said, looking dejected. "It probably would not have been a smart investment, anyway."

"That may be true. We don't always do things for money, though." Charley responded.

"I typically do. What else is there? Money gives one respect and power," said Mr. Collins. "It's a fact."

"I see. I certainly can agree that many people would consider that true, probably most in fact," Charley responded.

"That's all my wife sees in me. Money pays for her visits to the hair salon and weekends with her girlfriends. She couldn't care less who I was as long as I keep paying for her plastic cards. The only reason I married her was that she got pregnant. My dad called me a waste when he saw me drinking one afternoon at home when my mother came over to see the baby. My wife chimed in with an agreement. There was a blow-up, and I have not seen him since. I'm not sure why I am telling you this. I guess I know you won't be around much longer, anyway."

"I know why a man turns to drink or many other things to reduce pain. I also know how the feeling of being disrespected can turn into anger. It might even cause one to strike out at someone you love. It's not an excuse. However, it provides some insight into where the disease might be. Shame and anger can be like acid. Alcohol mixes to numb the acid while it eats whole through organs; heart, liver, or intestines—you don't always get to choose."

Mr. Collins responded. "I'm not sure if you're talking like a preacher or a doctor, Mr. Howard. Whom have you been talking with, Reverend Howard?"

"I met your father and mother because of a personal matter a few weeks back. I know your father is terminally ill. How do you feel about that?" Charley asked. He watched Walter's face as he showed softness around his eyes.

"Like a baseball hit me at top speed, and I need a drink to stop the pain." Mr. Collins said.

Charley gently continued. "You are sober now, so let out the truth without the booze. I'm just listening."

Walter had a flash of an image of himself, and he broke the thick shell he wore. His voice cracked, and he blurted, "I never meant to hit my mother that day. I never meant to destroy my relationship with my parents. There were so many things that made me angry growing up. I hated all the religious rules in our house. I wanted a bike for my birthday when I was six years old; that's all I wanted. I got the bike that I wanted. I was so proud of it, but rained that night, so I didn't get to ride the bike when my father rolled it into the dining room with the cake and candles. I had to wait till the next day. Unfortunately, my brother got home early because he had a dentist appointment. He took the bike out of the garage, rode it for a while, and left it in the yard. When my dad came home, he backed the truck up in the yard to unload some mulch. My bike crumbled under the weight of the back tires. I got blamed for leaving the bike out, and my brother said nothing. I was the one that got punished. My father never believed me. He cared more about hurting the truck than how I felt. His vehicle was more important than my broken heart. I did not get another until I was sixteen and paid for a new one with my earned money. I never asked for another present after that. That same year, I started working as a house painter for extra cash. After a couple of jobs, my father liked the idea and decided I needed to pay something back to help with household expenses. My father said it would help teach me to manage my money. I guess the concept sounded acceptable to him. However, he was taking over 80 percent of what I was making, and new things began appearing around the house, like his new circular saw and a new computer for his office. A dutiful son does not question authority, does he? My mother remained primarily quiet, and I began feeling more resentful, Reverend Howard."

"Sounds like some pretty powerful feelings to me. What would you like that 6-year-old and that 16-year-old boy to know?"

"I don't know." Walter looked down at his hands. "It's stupid, but I want to know that someone felt my pain through those years. I want to know that someone out there feels my disappointment."

"That's not stupid. It's human." Charley stated.

"You're not going to get religious on me, are you?" said Walter with a sneer.

"No, I'm not. I was listening, Mr. Collins. I'm an ordinary guy, just like you. Someone else was listening, though. Relationships take trust to build. My favorite place is walking along the sand and sea oats, as I feel God with me when he touches my face with sunshine and a sea breeze. I lost someone dear to me recently. I couldn't talk to my wife. She was hurting, too. And I couldn't speak to my colleagues as they might not completely understand the pain and, even worse, condemn and judge me. I almost threw life away with a shot of whiskey. The bottle was free as it had been a gift; imagine that. It was waiting for me in a closet as a bear waits for salmon on the falls. Chomp goes through my life in the claws of the bear. In my case, I cried out. Before I knew it, a frog appeared and poured the poison down the drain before it got too close."

"You are not making this up, are you?" asked Mr. Collins.

"No, I wasn't, even the frog part!" Charley looked up with a mischievous smile. "It's your choice. Since you brought up your father, would you like to see if you could visit him? My gut feeling is that he wants to see you and that you have been very much on his mind."

"Do you mean today?" Mr. Collins asked.

"I don't know if he is well enough, but you could find out. Why don't you call your mother first and start there?" Charley suggested.

With some hesitation, Mr. Collins took out his phone and looked back at Charley before he pressed his parents' home number. The call avoided being diverted to voice mail when his mother's voice answered. Mr. Collins sucked in the air before replying to the other end's voice. "Hello, Mother."

"Oh, my goodness! Wally, I can't believe it's your

voice. Where are you? Has something happened?" Mrs. Collins asked in disbelief. Her voice broke up through her tears.

"It's a long story, but I've been with Reverend Howard this afternoon and want to see Dad."

"Of course, Wally. He'll be sleeping for most of the afternoon. He is so much clearer in the morning. Can you come then? He is up around seven, and I do not give him his medication until ten. That makes him groggy again," Mrs. Collins informed her son. "He asks about you, Wally. Your father misses you very much!"

"Thank you, Mother." Walter choked up. "Yes, Mother, I will take the time to see him in the morning. Goodbye, Mother. I love you!" Walter said with his voice breaking and his mother's sobs being heard over the phone. Finally, Walter composed himself and turned toward Charley. "It was that easy?"

"Relationships are never easy," Charley responded. "Now, for what I called you about today. I am returning with my wife to Savannah in two weeks for good. If you want this space, I suggest calling Mr. Pratt before the end of this week. It will be completely back in his hands by then."

"Charles, I don't know what to say. I feel like I've just gone through a life-changing event this afternoon." Walter admitted.

Charley shook Mr. Collin's hand and got off the

stool to walk him to the door. "Good, but it's up to you. Having faith in a God is a courageous thing. There's no arrogance in God's way of doing things. It's a step in humility to lose control and talk with God daily to find your way." Charley said his goodbyes and closed the rented office one last time. He looked around and appreciated that the rental space looked more welcoming and cared for than when he found it. He dropped off the keys to the proprietor and drove back to the inn that evening, longing to be with his wife.

Ali had dinner ready with a table on the patio prepared for a meal outdoors that evening. She wanted to enjoy the last days at the inn. Charley enjoyed every moment by conversing on the side porch till nightfall and listening to things that mattered to Ali.

"Do you know I'm already lining up some leads on some local projects there when we settle in?" Ali said.

"When we married, we promised to work our lives into one. We never envisioned losing Michael after he had been a beacon. Michael grew up here and made this area his home. That tells me he was happy here." Charley responded.

"Michael was a child who would have been happy wherever people loved him. Maybe before he met you, he thought you did not love him. I never told him you didn't want him because I knew you never had the chance to know him. Maybe he disliked visiting Savannah before he knew the truth."

"I think you are right, Ali. I am thankful I had the time to be with him and show how much I loved him before leaving us. That was the most wonderful time of my life. I still feel him, though, even though he's gone. The things he cared about still matter to me. I grieve because I can't physically talk with him, but I'm not alone. I still have him with me. I thought it would be that I couldn't live with the loss, but somehow, I have found a peace that it is more of a hope that is excited for the time when I will see him again."

"You know, I feel the same way too, Charley. We haven't lost him. We can't see him, but I know he's still with us. Our son brought us together, even though he shortly left this place for another home. I can't explain it, but I feel comforted knowing there must have been a plan, and he was one of the beautiful threads in the tapestry. I am happy we are together, Charley, and can share this part of our lives. I wouldn't have known that there was so much more to life that I would have missed without you."

The next few days went by in a blur. By Saturday, all items were ready for relocation. While it was still dark outside, Ali wrote notes in her journal and tucked them away in her suitcase. Charley helped her load the last few things into her car.

"You give me the signal, and I will follow behind when you're ready," Charley said before kissing her forehead. He then walked back to the motorized camper and settled in.

"Charley, I'm ready to go!" Ali said on her phone as she pulled out of the drive for the last time. Bea found a place in the back seat of Ali's vehicle. Charley followed with Beaux curled on the soft bed placed on the passenger seat floor. The caravan sat out for the interstate, with the target being home.

"I don't think Charley noticed," said a woman wearing dark glasses, sitting in the front seat of a dark vehicle on the street without light posts in the pre-dawn hours.

"I don't think so either. Great job, kids!" said Bob, sitting behind the wheel. "He'll be slower than us. We will give him a head start and follow behind and see if we can meet up with them at his first stop."

"Not a problem, Dad. Those decals were adorable of a frog with his stick-figured family, Mom. That will let him know who was behind the soaping of his windows on the truck he is towing."

"Well, everybody, I think we are ready. Does everyone have enough legroom?" Bob asked.

All responded with "yes" in unison.

"Well then, let's head out of our stealth site here and begin our track as a southbound cruiser. The expected arrival of sunrise was somewhere in West Virginia. If I know Charley, he will have his radar for coffee somewhere south of the state line. With his rig, he will have to go in. However, we can remain incognito going through the drive-through after he comes out. We're on our way home now!" Bob said and put the vehicle in drive.

The first honk came about three hours at a drive-thru in West Virginia. Both passengers smiled and waved when their fifth-wheeler pulled around him after passing through the right-hand lane. Charley waved back and continued down the highway. He was more focused on keeping up with the white sedan in front of him. Charley was about to hit the Virginia border when he heard another honk. Several more honks were noted soon after from both the right and left. He was not sure what to make of it. Charley thought he should pull into the next rest stop when he reached the next stop and look at the vehicle he was driving and towing to be sure all was fine. He texted Ali about his intentions. Several travelers pulled off into the rest area, including a sizeable four-wheel drive with plates containing a peach in the center.

Charley pulled his vehicle into the larger slots where the truckers parked. He put Beaux's leash on, exited from the driver's side, and headed toward the grassy area. He soon joined up with Ali. After stretching their legs by taking a short walk, they strolled back to the motorized camper to get some refreshments for themselves and their pets. Charley then went walking around his vehicle to check on everything.

Ali heard Charley laugh and was quite curious. "What's going on?" Ali asked as she came around the corner. Ali looked up at Charley. "Oh, my goodness!" Ali read the sign out loud. *Recently married. Welcome home!* In the small corner were decals of one frog and four stick people. How did they do that?"

A voice came from a few yards away. "Well, it's about time you stopped for a break from the road. I was afraid I would have to come up with an emergency bathroom break for my crew here." Bob cried out. "That last stretch of highway with the grove of trees near the overlook sure was tempting. I wasn't sure there was a wide enough tree trunk for Carole," Bob teased. "She is more self-conscious than I am. I never could get her to moon anyone while we were dating."

"You all did this to my truck. Plus, you've been stalking us from Pennsylvania?" Charley incredulously asked as he reached over to give Bob a big hug and then one to Carole.

Bob gave a slight shrug of his shoulders. "The kids wanted to add a trail of cans, but I thought that might be a bit too much. The timing was perfect. The kids met some friends on the way hiking and traveled back with them as far as Pennsylvania. I told them I would pick them up. I met up with Darla and David just east of the address we found on the website for the inn. I used the address and the website to give me directions. We left early this morning from the hotel where Carole and I stayed last night and picked up the kids. I used Ali's web page to give me directions. Gail identified the inn immediately from a cover of one of Ali's books. It worked out perfectly." Bob responded.

Charley looked at Ali and laughed, "Your books sure get around." Then, giving attention to the two young adults who were present, Charley asked, "So, you made it to the end?"

"Not really, because the end of the trail was not our true destination. We were going to work in a computer camp for kids in Pennsylvania for a couple of weeks. We had a shuttle pick us up off the trail, and we had a family who was our host for the two weeks while we were there. The computer camp took place at a local private school. In the end, a group of us formed tight friendships."

"I want to hear all about that when we get back. I wouldn't complete a long-distance hike, but I sure would enjoy living through the experience vicariously through two young people like you. Did you have trail names?" Charley asked.

"It was so cool! And we have recorded some of the hike, so we'll be happy to have a snack night at the house and watch it all on Dad's big screen," Bob's daughter added. "David must get back, though, as he has an interview on Monday." She then turned, walked over, and crouched down to the sniffing and licking dogs. "So, this is Beaux's sister Bea. They are so cute! You must let us watch them when you are away, Charley."

"I will take you up on that, Darla, but the two together can be a barrel of trouble!" Charley added with a chuckle.

"It's going to be so good to have you both next door again," Carole chimed in. "Bob has been moping around the house without his best friend. We stopped and grabbed a couple of dozen donuts and bagels just down the road. Why don't you come on over and grab one? Bob will pull down the truck's gate, and we'll tailgate off the back before we head off."

Ali responded by making a request. "If Dave and Darla take these keys and get the cooler in my trunk, we'll have beverages. We have plenty of all kinds of drinks already on ice."

"Sure," piped up David, and walked Darla to the car.

"I think Charley and I both are eager to get back to Savannah," Ali responded while linking her arm with Charley's.

"We love hearing that!" Bob put in. Almost thirty minutes went by as the group fueled themselves on a traveler's feast and conversed about events of the past week. "I think we're going to pull out in a few minutes. We are planning on driving until we reach home today. I plan to arrive at about seven tonight. Now that we've caught up with you, we will let you go on at your own pace for the rest of the trip." said Bob.

"Sounds good. Call us if you get into trouble somewhere," Bob said, feeling warm in the cheeks. Charley and Ali walked back to their vehicles and made their plans for the rest of the trip.

Several hours later, the caravan of a car, motorhome, and truck in tow arrived at the quiet lane that

Charley called home. The Georgia skyline displayed the brilliance of scarlet, peach, and amber hues before the glowing globe in the west. The pups burned off their energy while walking around the neighborhood. Charley pointed out to Ali the area down by the private marina, where Charley stored a small sailboat. After that, Ali and Charley showered to refresh themselves from the long journey.

In the wee hours of the morning, husband and wife were still talking and digesting the last few months, sitting in Charley's favorite spot above the studio. From their perch, they could see the silvery surface of the ocean lit by the moon and the lighthouse beacon.

Charley commented. "We're watching the sunset simultaneously and in the same location. Was that ever one of your wishes?"

Ali shook her head, meaning "yes".

Charley took a deep breath before he responded. "I had the same dream, too."

Ali softly said, "It's perfect here tonight."

"Yes," Charley agreed as he popped another glazed pecan in his mouth. After a few seconds of silence, Charley looked at Ali and squeezed her tighter. "Happy Anniversary!"

Ali placed her shoulder on his chest, just close enough for him to lay his head. "It's not our anniversary, Charley. What made you say that?" Ali questioned.

"It's been six months, two days, and ten hours since we were married. I say that's an anniversary!"

"Men don't remember things like birthdays and wedding anniversaries, Charley," Ali teased.

"They do if they waited thirty-two years for his bride to say I do," Charley responded. "Now look up there in the sky. Pick out the brightest sky star shining on us this evening."

Ali followed his directions. "Okay, I pick that one to the right of the moon."

"I think it's that one, too. Do you know what else I think?" Charley asked. "I think Michael's smiling at us tonight from that star one, making sure we see the path back home."

"I like that thought, Charley. But that was only an idea in a story I wrote long ago."

"Perhaps, but I believe that there was more truth than fiction than you thought it to have."

"Really?" Ali questioned her husband as she continued to gaze out over the landscape.

"You gave me a seed of hope in that story when you gave me that gift. I didn't know I would need it until I almost lost the trail."

"You held my hope in your hands until I was ready to accept the love I never knew I could have in this life and the one to come. I know I will see Michael again and all the others who loved me along the way.

Epilogue

IT WAS TUESDAY MORNING, and three months had gone by since Charley returned to Savannah, resuming his church pastor duties. Coming in with his covered mug of coffee, he laid his computer down on his desk and pushed up his sweater sleeves to prepare for the papers that always seemed to pile up on his desk. His first appointment was in an hour, so Charley planned to put a dent in the stack of correspondence. One unexpected envelope caught his attention as he looked through the pile. Charley took the envelope from C. Pratt and addressed it to the church with his attention. Inside there was a sealed envelope addressed to the Reverend Charles Howard. Charley opened it and read the letter. Charley's smile grew wider as he read the contents. Mr. Pratt reported that shortly after Charley turned over the keys to the rental space, an offer came to buy the building for more than Mr. Pratt dreamed. The party was particularly interested in the rental that Charley had remodeled while he was there. Charley's read the note from his former landlord where it said he received an offer that was more than he would ever Imagen for the place. Since the deal closed last week, Mr. Pratt could retire with a substantial retirement account. He prayed and that his conscience would not be clear unless he shared a portion of the overflow from the sale. Charley's brows moved closer while sipping on his coffee. Mr. Pratt had signed two checks, one for the church as a gift and one written to Charles Howard for the time and labor he put into the rental. Charley read the rest of the comments. I wanted to ensure that I thanked you for the overflowing blessings I have received because of your talent and thoughtfulness. I cannot ignore the change it has made in me. It's as if I came alive again, Mr. Pratt wrote.

Mr. Pratt expressed his best wishes to Reverend Howard and his wife, the former Ali Taylor. He wanted to share a story about Ali. He wrote about his anniversary celebration at the inn two years ago. Ali had recalled why they were making the reservations, and she made sure there was a fresh bouquet on our table for my wife with a box of chocolate walnut brownies all packaged up in bows and ribbons to take home, courtesy of the innkeeper. That evening was one of Roxanna's most treasured memories, she told me later. Unfortunately, I lost my wife to a heart attack a few months later. I can never repay your wife for giving us that memory together.

Charley sat back and thought about that for a

moment before reading the last part of the letter. Mr. Pratt expressed his wish that he would like to come to the church where Reverend Howard is the pastor. He hadn't been to a Sunday church service in a long time, but Savannah sounded like a great place to start.

Charley slowly closed the envelope and smiled. He immediately tapped a message on his phone. *You are welcome anytime.*

Coastal Saga Series

Salty Beginnings

Burning Bush Bakery

Captain Bodacious

www.oceantimepublishing.com

About the Author

D.L. Barnes lives near Atlanta, Georgia. The Coastal Saga series was inspired by the natural beauty along the southern coast of Carolina and Georgia.